A BIKER
undone

A Nantucket Novel of Suspense

Charles E. Soule

ISBN: 1439270945
ISBN-13: 9781439270943

ACKNOWLEDGMENTS

My sincere thanks to my family and those many Nantucket friends who continually encouraged this second novel, and especially to those who found the time to read and comment on the manuscript: my wife, Elna; my daughter, Kimberly; my son, Chuck Jr.; my daughter-in-law, Pam, and my administrative assistant for more than thirty years, Ann LaBrie.

DEDICATION

To a very special group of individuals, the hundreds of home office and field associates of the Paul Revere Insurance Group, who supported and encouraged me throughout my more than forty years with the company.

AUTHOR'S NOTE

Having spent my entire business career in the home office of an insurance company that specialized in disability income insurance, I have some personal knowledge of the great temptation that lures some individuals to devise fraudulent schemes in hopes of illegally pocketing thousands of dollars. Although companies employ various methods to safeguard against fraud, there are always opportunities for unsavory individuals to take advantage of loopholes. The exact circumstances of the fraud scheme in this novel are entirely fictitious, and in fact, a student of the disability business will recognize that I have in some situations embellished the facts to enhance the story line.

I have lived on Nantucket for more than ten years and have the highest regard for the personnel of the Nantucket Police Department. None of the characters in this book resemble any person on the police force, past or present, and all of the circumstances developed in the plot are entirely fictitious.

October 2008

It was just turning dusk in the small New England town of Upton, Massachusetts, a distant suburb of Boston, and the bicyclist was closing in on her fifteen-mile ride. Allison Sheppard worked in a town outside of Boston, and she made it a practice of getting home early enough in the evening to get in her needed exercise at least three times during the work week. On the weekend she often took a ride at least twice as long, frequently with the bike club she belonged to. On this crisp early October evening, she had taken a route that took her through back country roads and into a small state park where the heavily wooded scenery was relaxing and offered the pleasant preview of early fall foliage. She was an experienced cyclist and had cycled regularly since she graduated from college some nine years before.

With about four miles remaining in her ride, she was cruising at a fast clip down a long straightaway, enjoying the force of the cool air on her face, with almost no traffic, when she heard a vehicle approaching from behind. She automatically steered her bike a little farther to the right side of the road, even though there were no cars approaching from the opposite direction, and therefore there was plenty of room for the car to pass her. As the car came abreast of her, it swerved sharply to the right, hitting the rear side of Allison's bike, and she lost control and went off the road into the nearby woods.

The car slowed for a moment, the driver observing the bicyclist through his rearview mirror as Allison lost control, and then the driver sped up and disappeared around the next corner.

More than an hour later, the sun having set and darkness capturing the wooded area, the driver of another car picked up the reflection of something in his headlights. As he slowed to get a clearer look, he noticed that it was a bicycle. He stopped and backed up to get a better look and at that point saw Allison lying among the trees. He rushed into the wooded area to find her unconscious, bleeding from her head, and with her helmet some distance away. He quickly returned to the car and called 911 on his cell phone.

The driver then returned to the injured bicyclist and tried to stop the bleeding from the head wound with pressure from a towel he had in his car. The injury looked severe to him, but he also knew that head injuries always seemed to bleed profusely. He also noticed that one of her legs was clearly twisted at an unnatural angle, but he did not dare to try to move her. Although it seemed like much longer, the police arrived within ten minutes and the ambulance shortly after. The medics examined Allison and gave her immediate first response aid, and she was transported to the nearest hospital in Framingham, some twelve miles away.

May 2003

Dick Gimble lounged in his small apartment, considering again the events over the past several months. The continuing bitterness of those events overshadowed any attempt he might have made to move on with his life.

His separation and divorce after seven years of marriage had been a financial nightmare. He did not regret the breakup with his wife, and if truth be known, he did not miss his two children all that much. His ex-wife had won custody, which he hadn't really resisted, and he found that seeing the children every other weekend more than filled his limited needs as a father. He enjoyed the physical fooling around with the kids, but his own personal life had always taken priority over his family. Indeed, although Dick did not accept or recognize this as one of the reasons his wife sought the divorce and custody, in the divorce proceedings it became quite evident that the arrival of the children presented demands on him that he was not ready or able to accept. He simply was not a good father or husband.

The financial settlement forced on him by the court, both child support and alimony, left him strapped and of necessity having to live a scaled-down lifestyle. His former wife, Carol, had not worked since their first child was born five years before, and the fact that she had no job or other income figured largely in the court's decision to award what Dick considered outrageous alimony payments. She continued to live in the house they had purchased four years before, but he was still responsible for the mortgage payments. When everything was finally settled, including the exorbitant attorney's fees, Dick could afford only this small apartment for himself, and even that was a stretch. It was furnished sparsely and principally with secondhand furniture. It never occurred to Dick that Carol was also subsisting on less household income than before the divorce—trying to stretch one income to now support two households placed limits on both of their lifestyles.

And then came the other disappointment, no, the real injustice, of being passed over at work for the assistant manager's position in the claim department. Dick had joined JAIC, the John Adams Insurance Company, right after finishing college, and after a short training period he had been assigned to the Disability Income Claim Department as a claim examiner. He was energetic and bright, and early in his career he demonstrated both an ability to quickly learn the rules and procedures of the job as well as a clear ambition to take on more responsibility and move ahead. Two years previously he had been promoted to senior claim examiner, a position that reflected the fact that he had mastered the profession in a relatively short period of time. When the assistant manager's position became open a few months earlier, he felt quite confident that he was the best candidate. He was indeed a hard worker, one who was early on the job and stayed after closing time when there was still outstanding work to be done. He truly enjoyed the responsibilities of the claim examiner, the investigative nature of the work to determine if an individual was legitimately disabled and eligible for benefit payments. He felt a great satisfaction when he found a claimant trying to extend the disability income benefits beyond the point where the person was still truly disabled. He had always liked mysteries and intrigue and found that the investigative work of his job allowed him to play at being a detective. He was, in fact, considered a good young examiner by his management.

However, when it came time to fill the open position, Dick clearly lacked the other qualities that were important in a good manager. He was not particularly well liked by his peers since he displayed an attitude of always knowing a little more than anyone else. He was quick to point out someone else's faults, and his personal ambition was a little too transparent. He was one of those people who wanted to make certain everyone knew just how good he was, but he didn't have the personal skills to know how much he irritated others.

And so, both the divorce and being passed over for the promotion had happened within a few months of each other. The fact that the promotion would have meant more income for Dick, at a time when he clearly needed it, made the disappointment that much more personal and difficult to accept. An additional thousand dollars a month of income would have eased the financial burden, even though money alone would not have alleviated Dick's long-term bitterness over the divorce.

One of the few friends he had made at the company was an underwriter who worked out at the same athletic club that Dick did. Ed Fletcher had quite a different personality than Dick. He had been at the company for almost fifteen years, and he showed little ambition to move beyond his present position. On the other hand, they both shared the unpleasant characteristic of being quick to criticize the faults of others while not recognizing their own shortcomings. Over the years, Ed had become especially critical of his boss. He tended to be somewhat lazy, arriving at work a little after the scheduled start time and always leaving precisely at closing time. Frequently there were requirements in the underwriting department to have underwriters put in overtime because of heavy workloads; however, when Ed's boss asked him to put in that overtime, he frequently invented an excuse to avoid it. The relationship between Ed and his boss was stressed with their business interests and personalities being so different, and Ed came to believe that his boss had it in for him, and he frequently complained to Dick.

In most ways Ed and Dick were indeed strange bedfellows, both enjoying the negativism in the other, and if you were to listen in to their conversation, it usually involved a critical discussion of others. Where most men would tend to discuss sports, politics, or some project they were working on at home, Dick and Ed seemed to build up their own egos and become energized through criticizing their family or business associates.

On this particular day, Dick and Ed were at a pub enjoying a beer after working out. Dick began to complain about the company's procedures as to how it investigated people who were submitting a disability claim for income replacement payments. He said that many of the procedures were lax and there were loopholes that a fraudulent claimant could take advantage of. He said, emotionally, "The company is losing millions of dollars each year in making disability payments to people who aren't really disabled but are looking for an easy buck."

Ed tried to give him some resistance. "Oh, come on, Dick, you're exaggerating."

That only spurred Dick on further.

"There are policyholders who are smart enough to know these loopholes. Some claimants start out with a legitimate disability, but then they continue claiming they're disabled even after they can return to work. I've seen others who fake the claim from the start. I'm always on the lookout for those guys, but I can tell you that most of the examiners aren't smart enough to recognize them. Part of the problem is the work load. Since there aren't enough examiners to handle the increased numbers of claims, most of them end up taking shortcuts and not looking for those kinds of frauds. They're frankly lazy and don't give a damn. Even some of the managers either don't know or don't care. I know I could personally make thousands of dollars easily by just working those loopholes."

"Oh, come on, Dick, now you're really stretching it."

"The hell I am. It's easy to fake a disability. As a matter of fact, I'm talking hundreds of thousands, maybe millions, not just a few thousand."

"I still think you're dreaming. What are you going to do, send in a phony application and then a phony claim on top of it?"

"Sure, why not?"

"You're forgetting that applicants have to go through the underwriting investigation to get their policies approved before they can even submit a fraudulent claim."

"How much do you want to bet I could do it?"

"You're crazy."

"How about a thousand dollars?"

"I don't have that kind of money to throw around."

"Tell you what. I'm going to do it just to prove it to you, and at the same time I'll get the personal satisfaction of screwing the company. Don't ask me anything more about this for a couple of months, but by the end of July, I'll show you a claim check from the company."

Ed shook his head, not really believing that Dick would go ahead with his scheme but knowing it was foolish to argue with him any further.

October 2008

Jack Kendrick was truly enjoying his photograph gallery business in Quincy Market, the retail store he had created and opened some three years before with the money he had earned from selling his photographs of the terrorist attack that occurred only a few yards from where his business was now located. Occasionally he looked over at Faneuil Hall, remembering that day when the explosion occurred and when he was right outside with the WBOS television crew recording the events. The pictures he took that day that earned him the hundred thousand dollars were not those taken with the TV video camera, but rather the candid shots he had taken with his own digital camera. He was the only one who had captured many of the pictures, including the one of the terrorist leaving the area. What a lucky break for him to have been at this location at such an opportune time, and as a result he got the funds he needed to open up this photography business that he and Amy had dreamed about for years.

Even though he was still learning the intricacies and fine points of running this kind of retail business, the first two years had shown steady growth in both customers and income. He was working long hours, but the personal satisfaction obtained from being his own boss more than made up for the hours he put in. Amy had been very supportive and encouraged him all along the way. Once a week, sometimes twice, they would switch jobs and she would come and look after the store while he played the role of stay-at-home dad. It was a good break for both of them from their regular routines, and more importantly, it gave Jack some time to spend with his rapidly growing children.

Although over the years Jack had taken thousands of still photographs of various subjects, mostly around New England, he took time to continue to take more photos and add to his portfolio. He was a perfectionist and found that he would throw away several dozen before selecting one that he felt deserved to be reproduced and displayed in the store. He found that his customers preferred those shots of everyday human interest types of situations. Catching subjects when they were not aware of being photographed was a challenge, but it always presented the best results. From experimenting many years ago, he knew that trying to stage a scene always lacked something in the final product. There was simply something artificial that just couldn't be hidden.

He had found many of his photo opportunities right in the city, and indeed some of his best photos had been taken around the old market buildings in the Quincy Market area. There was always something interesting to observe and catch on film with the thousands of people who passed through the market area daily.

The entertainers who performed in front of the middle building in the market—jugglers, musicians, magicians, mimes, gymnasts—frequently were fascinating subjects to capture, and especially the reactions of children to the entertainment. Tourists, businesspeople passing through the market, and sailors off their ship for a day of liberty all were potential photo targets if he could catch them off guard. On a pedestrian mall between two of the market buildings is a bench with a life-size bronze statue of Red Auerbach, the famous coach of the Boston Celtics, holding the traditional victory cigar in his hand. Jack had numerous photos of visitors sitting on the bench as if in conversation with the coach.

An avid sports fan, Jack attended Patriots, Red Sox, Celtics, or Bruins games several times a year. In recent years he had even taken up following the Revolution, the area professional soccer team. Some of his best photos of athletic events were not of the contests themselves, but rather candid shots of the players on the sidelines, reacting to a play on the field, or interacting with a fan. Bostonians and New Englanders are avid sports fans, and he found that those prints went over well with the public. The fact that the Red Sox had won two World Series, the Patriots three Super Bowls, and the Celtics a World Championship, all since the year 2000, undoubtedly contributed to the demand. Even though the Boston Bruins hockey team had not won a championship in recent years, their fans were legendary in their fanatic loyalty. Boston fans had truly been spoiled in recent years with the success of its sports teams; their expectation for repeat performances frequently exceeded reasonable expectations. But it was certainly good for Jack's business.

On those days when Amy took over the shop and he was with the children, he'd frequently take them along on a photo excursion. After a heavy snowstorm, he'd head out into the country to catch some of those special winter scenes found in New England. In the fall he'd take a ride into the Berkshires, or north into New

Hampshire or Vermont, at the peak foliage time, and these prints were always popular ones. Many of his shots were taken of Boston Harbor and along the seacoast, both north and south of the city. The area offered an endless variety of scenic photo opportunities and all within a few hours' drive from Boston.

And within the city itself there were literally dozens of historic sites that visitors and residents alike wanted to remember with a photograph. The Freedom Trail wove its way from the gold-domed current State House to the Old South Meeting House, where the Boston Tea Party was planned, to the Old State House where the Declaration of Independence was originally read, to Faneuil Hall, to Paul Revere's house, to the Old North Church, and to the battleship Old Ironsides. All were popular sale items in Jack's shop. The Boston area was loaded with other Revolutionary War subjects—the Lexington Green where the first shots were fired on April 18, 1776, the Concord Bridge, and Bunker Hill. One of his most popular photos was of the frozen lagoon in the Public Garden in February, the recent snowfall still hanging on the tree branches. Many people came into his shop and could take a tour of Boston's history just by looking through the accumulation of photos Jack had taken over the years. Even though these were still pictures with fixed subjects, Jack was continually taking additional shots to try to improve upon the subject—a little different angle, an improved lighting or shadowing, a different season of the year.

On occasion he'd drive up the rugged Maine coast and look for the ideal photo situation on the rocky shore. He had purchased small cameras for Natalie and Jeremy, and they enjoyed playing photographer along with Jack. A few weeks before, he had taken one of each of their pictures that they were especially proud of, enlarged them, and put them in fancy frames. They now proudly hung in their bedrooms.

In the summer they continued to vacation at Amy's parents' summerhouse on Nantucket, and this opened up a whole additional arena for pictures. He found that prints of the island's three lighthouses were especially popular, including a winter scene of the Brant Point Lighthouse that found frequent buyers. Up and down cobblestoned Main Street there were additional photo opportunities of historic buildings and quaint shops. Sailboats, windsurfers, surfboarders, boaters, sandcastle builders, street vendors, sunbathers, and almost any vacation situation were all frequent subjects for Jack. Photos of the Oldest House, the Old Windmill, and the sunsets taken from Step Beach were ones that were continually in demand. He never left the house without at least one camera, and he rarely returned without having taken at least a dozen or two photos. It used to be only a hobby with him, and even though it was now his business, he was diligent at it, and the enjoyment and satisfaction never left him. He was truly a lucky man to have been able to turn his avocation into his vocation.

Occasionally he would think back to that time when he first became entangled in the series of events leading up to the terrorist incident at Faneuil Hall and the subsequent capturing on film of the participants on the steamship ferry on the trip to Nantucket. He never failed to notice the porthole on the ferry where the terrorist had tried to escape his pursuer and ended up drowning.

Ed Fletcher had truly forgotten about Dick Gimble's boasting that he could submit a fraudulent disability claim to their company without getting caught, but true to his word, one day after work some two months later, Dick showed Ed a claim check for a thousand dollars. He was really gloating over the fast one he'd pulled on the company.

Ed examined the check and said, "Dick, who the hell is Philip Costa?"

"Oh, he's the policyholder that I used to submit the claim."

Ed thought for a minute. "But how did you get a policy issued?"

Dick, with a sly smirk on his face, said, "Well, there are a lot of ways to do that, but I simply went into our records and picked a policy that had been approved a couple of years ago and had subsequently lapsed for nonpayment of premium. I paid the premium to reinstate the policy a couple of months ago, right after we talked. Then a few weeks later I submitted a claim for two weeks of disability payments for a broken wrist. The claim department doesn't really investigate any short-term accident claims. I changed the address to a post office box number so any correspondence and the claim check would come directly to me. I only had to pay a hundred-and-twenty-dollar monthly premium to reinstate the policy, and now I'll just let it lapse again. No one will ever know the difference."

"Boy, you're taking a big risk that someone will find out. Supposing this guy, Costa, contacts the company to reinstate the policy himself?"

"The odds of that happening are pretty slim. I picked a policy where the policyholder had received the final lapse notice and hadn't replied."

"Did you submit a fake reinstatement form?"

"Well, yeah. I got a blank form, filled it out, and signed Costa's name and sent it in."

"Jesus, Dick, you're really playing with fire. What if you get caught?"

"It'll never happen. Look, the claim is now closed. Like I said before, I purposely only submitted it for two weeks of disability payments. No one ever looks at short-term claims for small amounts like that unless the same guy is submitting claim after claim, and this guy Costa isn't going to have any more claims."

"How about the physician's statement to certify that this guy really had a broken wrist?"

"Hell, I just picked a physician's name out of the telephone book and forged his name. They'll never check because the claim is so small."

So what are you going to do with the check?"

"Hell, I'm going to cash it. Otherwise the company will hassle me for not cashing it."

Ed hesitated for a minute and said, "Boy, you're really crazy, Dick. I couldn't take that risk."

"Look, Ed, I keep telling you there's no risk. The company is focusing all of its claim examinations on really large monthly payments, like more than four thousand dollars a month and claims that have lasted for three months or longer. That's where they think they're most vulnerable to losing big dollars from fraud. Someone who has a smaller claim and only a few weeks of disability is pretty much ignored. The company feels it's too costly to spend time and money on something that doesn't promise big returns. That's what I was trying to tell you a couple of months ago. There are really dozens of loopholes if you know how company procedures work."

"How many of these phony claims are there?"

"Oh hell, I don't know. But I can tell you that I find at least one a month where the claimant was either not disabled at all or was trying to extend his disability payments even though he was healthy enough to go back to work. You know, when someone doesn't like his job or is about to lose it, there's an incentive for him to fake a disability in order to get some money."

"I can't believe that the claim examiners aren't on the lookout for these kinds of situations."

"I told you before; we don't have enough examiners to fool around with the smaller claims. We're trained not to worry about those short claims that only amount to a few thousand when the really big bucks are those claims that are going to last for months or years and may total up to tens or even hundreds of thousands of dollars. Look, a policy that pays five thousand dollars a month adds up to sixty thousand dollars a year and could total well over a million dollars for someone who ends up disabled for life. That's where the big money is to be saved."

"Yeah, I know. But still it seems goddamn sloppy if we're leaving ourselves so open to fraud."

Dick shrugged his shoulders, put the thousand-dollar claim check back in his pocket, and said, "Well, whatever, but I can tell you this money's going to come in handy. Too bad I couldn't get one of these every month."

October 2008

Allison Sheppard was rushed into the emergency room at the hospital, and a triage team immediately began to assess and work on her multiple injuries. Although the compound fracture of the tibia and the dislocated shoulder were serious enough injuries, their principal concern was the head injury that had rendered Allison unconscious. It was apparent that the helmet she had been wearing had come off or become dislodged, and her head must have hit a tree. The examination of her skull showed a depressed fracture, and residue from the bark of the tree was embedded in her hair and skull. She had not regained consciousness since the accident.

After making the initial assessment and taking steps to stabilize the patient, the triage team determined that the injury was clearly serious enough for Allison to be transported as soon as possible to Massachusetts General Hospital in Boston. Their trauma center was considered one of the best in New England, and the Middlesex Hospital was simply too small to provide the level of services that would undoubtedly be necessary. The neurosurgical department at Mass General was rated as one of the best in the country, and it appeared that the patient would probably need surgery to deal with subdural bleeding and the depressed skull fracture.

A helicopter was dispatched from Boston, and Allison was transferred to the Boston hospital less than two hours from the time of the accident.

Allison was in her early thirties and had been employed at the John Adams Insurance Company in Newton, Massachusetts, a suburb of Boston located at the intersection of the busy Route 128 and Route 9. She had joined the company as an actuarial trainee after finishing graduate school, and she found her life was extremely busy with the demands of her chosen profession, especially the constant requirements of studying for the exams to be certified as a fellow of the Society of Actuaries. She had chuckled to herself over the word "fellow" that certainly underscored the male dominance of the profession in the past. However, in the twenty-first century many of the actuarial students were women, and it was a career that had interested Allison from her early years as an undergraduate in college.

She had always enjoyed mathematics and had been exceedingly good at it from an early age in grade school. She found herself in honors math courses from the time she entered high school, and the challenge of the more advanced courses, such as calculus and statistics, increased her interest and satisfaction. It never bothered her that few other women selected math as their college major, and although some of her friends might consider her a little too bookish, she was very comfortable in her own skin.

She had always been somewhat of a loner with only a few close friends, and she found great strength and satisfaction in the solitude of doing things on her own. She loved to read, and from an early age she had consumed books at a rate that was unusual. As a result, her advanced reading skills had always helped her to perform at a high level academically. She had been moderately successful at athletics, and here again her personality dictated the type of sports that interested her. She had been on the track team in high school and experimented with several different events; however, although she did well in short-distance runs, she found that the longer distances were truly her preference.

In college she had continued to pursue her running and lettered in cross-country all four years. She found great solace and strength in the "high" of the runner—that special feeling of being within herself as her legs moved her body and she felt the steady breeze in her face from the motion. She was especially energized during the fall cross-country season when the weather in the Northeast was cool and invigorating.

The ten actuarial exams a student had to complete before being certified as a fellow typically took several years to finish. Some actuarial students attempted to take two each year, and it was common for students to fail at least one exam along the process. They would then have to take it again and, in some instances, repeat the course several times. They were primarily courses you studied on your own, but in large companies a number of students might study together. Once you had completed the first five courses, you were designated an associate actuary, which usually carried with it an increase in salary and frequently more responsibility.

Since she joined the company, Allison had completed the first five courses without any difficulty, and a year previously she had been promoted and assigned to the disability income department in the company. The John Adams Insurance Company was one of the largest insurers in New England and was principally a life insurance company. Its disability insurance product line was much smaller in premium volume, but it was still ranked as one of the five largest disability insurers nationally.

Allison was somewhat apprehensive when she was assigned to the disability product; she was concerned that her advancement opportunities might be limited since it was one of the smaller product lines in her company. However, she was assured by her boss that this was not a permanent assignment and that she should consider it part of her development and training. Once she got involved in the details of the product, the pricing, the valuation, and the analysis of claim results, she saw there were certain advantages over the other product lines. Because she was the only actuary assigned full time to the product, she found that she had broader responsibilities than those actuaries in the larger product lines who tended to be given more narrow functions.

She had continued to spend considerable time studying for the remainder of her exams, which were more demanding and more difficult than the earlier exams, and this commitment along with the demands of her new responsibilities left little time for her social life. She had a few close friends but no serious involvement with the opposite sex, and her personality was such that at this point in her career she was quite satisfied with her life.

On the day after the injury, pressure began to build in her skull from the subdural hematoma, and it was necessary to perform surgery to relieve the pressure on her brain caused by the buildup of blood. She was still in a coma ten days after the accident; however, her vital brain activity showed no apparent long-lasting damage. Both her compound-fractured tibia and her shoulder required extensive surgical repair. The principal concern of her medical team, however, was the brain injury, how long she would remain in a comatose state, and whether she would have any residual effects from the severity of the brain injury.

Back in the town of Upton, where the accident occurred, there had not been any extensive investigation of the accident since there were no witnesses and no evidence from the damaged bicycle that an automobile had been involved. The only witness to the hit-and-run incident, Allison, was unable to provide any information.

November 2008

Jack and Amy Kendrick lived in the town of Quincy, a few miles south of Boston on the coast. Amy was busy with their two small children and with the one-day-a-week commitment to managing the photography store while Jack stayed at home with the children. She also shared the business load as the bookkeeper, a job that she was able to do at home and free Jack from this additional task and the expense of hiring a bookkeeper.

She received a telephone call from Allison's mother the day after she was injured. Amy and Allison had been roommates in college, had become very close friends, and had stayed in constant contact after graduation. Allison frequently came to Quincy on weekends, and the two children welcomed her as one of the family, calling her Auntie Al. Since neither Amy nor Allison had any siblings, the auntie label and role was a natural one. In fact, spending time with the Kendricks afforded Allison one of her few escapes from the demands of her career. They were truly like sisters, spoke to each other over the phone at least once each week, and were comfortable sharing the personal joys and concerns that close friends always do.

During the week following the accident, Amy spent many hours daily in the hospital at Allison's side, waiting for her to come out of the coma, frequently speaking to her in hopes of stimulating her subconscious, and praying for her complete recovery. It was perhaps one of the longest weeks of Amy's life, and as the days went by, everyone became concerned about Allison's lingering unconscious state. The physicians tried to assure Allison's parents and Amy that it was not uncommon after a severe head injury for the patient to remain unconscious for several days or even weeks. However, Amy had read enough about head injuries and comas to know that the longer Allison remained unconscious, the greater the likelihood that it might be permanent or that she would have some residual brain damage.

Allison's family and Amy were emotionally traumatized as they observed this formerly athletic, vibrant person lying lifeless in a hospital bed, her head bandaged from the surgery, her shoulder bandaged and in a sling, and her leg in a cast. It was a constant reminder of how fleeting life could be. As the days passed into the second and then the third week, and even though her vital signs remained normal, it was obvious that the physicians themselves were becoming concerned. Amy had to face the reality that the coma might last indefinitely, and she had to get back to her family and business responsibilities. She arranged her schedule so that she spent two days a week at the hospital, alternating with Allison's family.

On the twenty-third day of the coma, Allison began to show some signs of brief consciousness; her eyes fluttered and she demonstrated increased movement in her limbs. Finally on the twenty-sixth day she actually regained consciousness and was able to speak a few words. She was still heavily medicated, and she frequently lapsed into sleep. With each passing day, however, her periods of consciousness lengthened and her speech became more lucid and improved significantly. She recognized everyone in her family and, of course, Amy. There appeared to be no impairment in her speech or her mental capacity other than that caused by the medications.

She complained of a headache, not surprising given the severity of her injury, and after several days she had more and more questions. "Where am I? How did I get here? How long have I been here? What's the matter with my shoulder and my leg? How long was I unconscious? How serious is my head injury? When can I go home?"

Whoever was with her during these moments would attempt to answer the questions without alarming her, and the physicians stressed the importance of not staying too long during each visit so as to give Allison more time to rest, to heal, and regain her strength. They told Allison's parents that she would need to remain in the hospital under close monitoring for several more weeks and then would be sent to a rehabilitation center where she would likely spend at least two more months regaining her strength, the use of her limbs, and undergoing continual monitoring to determine if and how much brain damage had occurred. Even though her mental capacity was not impaired, there was still the possibility that some of her motor functions had been damaged.

Initially, Allison could not remember any specifics regarding the accident or even that she had been riding her bike. However, as the days and weeks passed, she began to recall a few details—that she had been riding her bike and where the accident occurred. It wasn't until the sixth week following the accident that one day she said to Amy, "I'm pretty certain that I was forced off the road by a car coming up from behind me. I remember hearing a car engine, and I consciously steered the bike over to the right side of the road; I'm certain I would have given plenty of room for any car to pass. It wasn't dark, and then I must have been hit. I don't really remember any more. I don't recall losing control, going off the road, or hitting a tree. The doctors tell me that it's normal for people not to remember the details of an accident and that I'm recalling more than most."

Amy asked, "When did you begin to remember this, Allison?"

"Well it's sort of come back to me in bits and pieces. I didn't want to say anything until I was sure of what I remembered. However, every day it seems to become clearer and clearer." She hesitated and then continued, "I haven't told my parents because I don't want to alarm them. I don't understand how someone could have hit me and not know it."

Amy hesitated and then said, "Well, you know that clears up something that's been bothering me. You're an excellent biker, and you must have been on that route more than a hundred times—I just couldn't understand how you could have gone off the road. I've wondered whether there was something in the road that you hit or if an animal jumped out in front of you and you lost control. Even though it happened at dusk, it was a clear day, there was still some light, you were on a straightaway, and you're a careful biker."

"Yeah, those questions have bothered me since I was first told how I was injured. I know I wasn't traveling at a reckless speed. I know the road was dry, and I've been through that park so often that I know every bump and crack in the road. I don't recall anything that would have caused me to lose control of the bike." Allison paused for a moment. "I don't understand why the driver didn't stop. You've told me that when the person found me it was probably at least an hour after the accident and that it was then dark, so it's got to be someone else who hit me."

"Well, I can't believe whoever it was didn't know he had hit you. It sounds like a typical hit-and-run; whoever it was just didn't want to get involved since they were personally responsible. Perhaps it was a young kid."

"I don't know. I can't imagine someone leaving an injured person by the side of the road, especially when they'd caused the accident."

"Allison, do you remember any details about the car?"

"No, I've tried to, but I can't recall anything yet."

"But you've said several times that it was a car, not a truck. So you do remember something about the vehicle?"

Allison paused before she said, "Yeah, it's a little fuzzy, but I'm quite certain it was a car, and the only other thing that keeps coming into my mind is the color green. I don't know whether that's anything or if I'm beginning to push too hard for details. The whole thing happened so fast that I didn't have time to pick out the make of the car or anything like that."

"Allison, I think you should go to the police. There may be some markings on the bike where it hit you. I've read that the police can identify the make of a vehicle by examining a piece of paint."

"Where's the bike now?"

"I'm not sure. I think I remember hearing someone say that the police department had it and would keep it until they were told what to do with it. I know it was pretty badly banged up, but I don't know whether it can be repaired."

"Would you call the police and find out if they still have it?"

"Sure, I'll do that as soon as I leave here. Do you want me to mention to them that you now remember being hit?"

Allison replied, "No, just find out if the bike's there. Give me a chance to see if I remember anything more in the next few days."

"OK, OK, and I won't mention anything to anyone else."

"Thanks, Amy. Thanks for everything and for being at my side all this time. I know this has screwed up your life for the last several weeks and taken you away from the kids."

Amy bent over and kissed Allison. "You're my best friend, almost my sister, and you know you'd do the same and more for me."

December 2003

It was a Friday evening, the last week in December, and Dick Gimble and Ed Fletcher were again enjoying a beer after work. They had been discussing their New Year's plans and the fact that the Patriots' last regular season game would be on Sunday.

Dick said, "Well, at least they've made the playoffs, but it's probably too much to expect they can go all the way. One Super Bowl in my lifetime is probably all I can hope for."

"Well, who knows? No one expected they'd win the first one. They've got a more experienced team this year, and Brady's got a couple of more years under his belt."

"Yeah, we'll see. Are you still on for New Year's Eve?"

"Sure. I went to First Night in Boston once before, and it was really a blast—parades, fireworks, music, thousands of people."

"Sounds like the kind of party we could really get into."

"Yeah, and on top of that the only cost will be the booze. We don't have to buy the First Night badges unless we plan to go into one of the venues, and I think there's plenty to do outside."

"OK, money's really short for me right now, so that sounds good."

Ed replied, "Tell me about it! I'm really strapped, and Christmas has me just about maxed out on two credit cards. The monthly payments are really getting to be a problem, and this month is going to be the worst yet."

Dick thought for a minute and said, "You complain about the credit cards all the time, and it just seems to be getting worse. Why don't you do something about it?"

"Like what? You mean stop living?"

"Either you've got to stop feeding your expensive tastes, or find some money somewhere. Look at my situation. I've had to cut back on just about everything in order to keep up with the child support and the goddamn alimony payments. My car is five years old while you're driving around in a new one. I don't know when I'll be able to afford a new one."

"Yeah, we've both got money problems, and the New Year doesn't look any better. My raises the last couple of years have been almost nothing. Each year I've lost pace with the cost of living."

Dick paused, stared at Ed for an unusual length of time, and then said, "Maybe there's a way to ease the problem for both of us."

"Sure, what are we going to do, rob a bank?"

"No, but a time comes in everyone's life when they have to take a bit of a risk if things are going to get any better. Maybe that time is now."

"What are you talking about?"

Dick hesitated again before continuing. Although this had been in his mind for several weeks, he knew that how he handled the next few minutes would determine if his plan went any further. He looked directly at Ed and said, "Well, I've been giving a lot of thought to my little experiment last summer with the phony claim. I think it's something that can really work on a bigger scale."

Ed looked up from his beer, stared at Dick, and said skeptically, "What are you talking about?"

"I'm actually serious. I really think it's a way to solve some of our problems."

"You've gotta be kidding. You got away with that once, but you were lucky."

"I don't think it was luck, Ed. I know the claim practices as well or better than anyone else, and I know where the big loopholes are if you look carefully."

"Jesus Christ, you're crazy, Dick."

"No, I'm not crazy; I'm just ready to get what I think ought to be coming to me. I'm sick of working my ass off for the company and not having them appreciate it."

"Well I'm sick of my job too, but I'm not ready to do something foolish and end up being fired or even in jail."

"Look, maybe I am crazy, but just hear me out. I've been working at the company for almost ten years, and you've been there longer than that. We've both been passed over for promotions, and we know our salaries are about at the max for the jobs we're in. I'm tired of having to scrimp on everything I need. I've never had much credit card debt, but with the alimony payments I can't survive without using the credit card. I'm digging a bigger hole for myself every month. What really pisses me off is that I know I handle a lot more claims every day than most of the other examiners, and on top of that I know I'm a better examiner—I'm saving the company tens of thousands of dollars every month. A lot of the other examiners are simply incompetent. They're just putting in the hours to pick up a paycheck. My salary doesn't at all reflect the job I'm doing."

Ed replied, "I know what you mean. I know I'm about maxed out at my salary, and I know that some of the newer underwriters are starting at salaries that are close to mine. I'm not being paid what I'm really worth either. On top of that, I have to put up with a boss who's a son of a bitch and continually hassles me."

"Ed, I know there's some risk in what I'm talking about, but frankly, I'm desperate. Just hear me out. Let's pretend this is sort of a game of 'what if?'"

Ed looked carefully at Dick and said, "OK, go ahead and play let's pretend, but it still sounds crazy to me."

"Well, ever since the phony claim I sent in last summer, I've been thinking about other loopholes. The one I used was to pay a premium on a lapsed policy and then submit a phony short-term claim on that policy. Then I let the policy lapse again. That approach works pretty well, but there are only a limited number of lapsed policies that would fit the profile of the kind of case I need. So I began thinking of exactly what would be the profile of the kind of new policy that would slip through the loopholes. For example, if we were to submit fictitious applications, we'd want to make certain that there wouldn't be any underwriting investigation. An application on a person in their midthirties with minimal or no medical history would not be unusual; however, one on a fifty-year-old with no medical history would be suspicious. So the odds of the fifty-year-old being checked out further by the underwriter are a lot greater than for a thirty-year-old. Similarly an app for a thousand dollars or two thousand dollars per month of indemnity would not trigger additional income investigation, where one for five thousand dollars would. There are other criteria that would minimize the chance of investigation—applications for short benefit periods carry less risk for the company than those where the benefits might be paid for years or for a lifetime; applications that have at least a thirty-day waiting period before payments begin eliminate a lot of short-term disabilities. There are a number of other criteria that would reduce the chance of investigation even further."

"Yeah, you're right that the application you describe would probably blow through underwriting without any additional investigation. But there are a lot of things you haven't covered. A licensed agent has to sign and submit the application. How do you handle that? And how about all of the information needed to set up the policy record—address for billing, bank information?"

"Well, I've thought about that, and I'd set it up so that all of these applications were done over the Internet through the new paperless application system. You need to help me out here because you're familiar with all of the new underwriting guidelines and I'm not. But there's no agent involved here since the application comes in directly over the Internet. If the application is for accident-only coverage and not for sickness, and has the other criteria I've mentioned, wouldn't that slip on through?"

Ed thought for a few moments and replied, "Yeah, it probably would. I hadn't thought about using the Internet system."

"Well, you've got to get into the twenty-first century, Ed. As far as the address for correspondence and billing, why not use one of those for-profit private post office boxes that have sprung up all over the country, you know like Mailboxes Etc.? As far as bank information is concerned, all you need to do is give the company a bank routing number and an account number. The premiums could be automatically taken out of the bank account, and the claim payments could be made directly into the same account."

"Dick, I see where you're headed, but there's got to be a lot more details you haven't thought of."

"You're probably right, but I think with some careful planning it can be done." He paused for a few seconds and then said, "Look, I'd like to make a trial run and see if it works. Will you help me out on the underwriting side?"

Ed stared at Dick and hesitatingly said, "I guess if you're still playing this as a game, then I don't mind helping you out by going a little further, but I don't want to get involved beyond that."

"OK, let me check out some things, put the parameters of the profile down on paper, and then get back to you, say sometime next week. In the meantime, you can be giving some thought from an underwriter's point of view as to what more needs to be considered in the profile."

"Yeah, I'll give it some thought, but you have to know that I still think the whole scheme is crazy."

"I hear you, and maybe it is. On the other hand, I think it's worth some further thinking and making a sort of test run. It may be the answer to both of our financial problems."

Dick was by nature a risk taker; he enjoyed sailing close to the wind. He was one of those people who always seemed to land on their feet, even after getting involved in something that was contrary to accepted societal standards and ethics or was borderline illegal. He was able to get away with it when others might be caught. Even back in high school when he worked in a small food market, he found that he could occasionally swipe a twenty-dollar bill from the cash register without ever raising any real suspicions. He had convinced himself, *The trick is to do it only now and then. If I do it too often, then I may get caught.*

He had gone to a small local college and found that there were ways he could cut corners and fool the professors. The Internet provided hundreds of sources for taking shortcuts in completing course assignments. There were times when his "research" for writing a paper involved going online and copying from some source major parts of the paper he finally submitted. On one occasion he was able to locate the questions for a final exam by accessing a professor's own computer program. The trick was not to do things so frequently that it became a pattern that someone might detect. Over a long period of years, his personal ethical standards had continually eroded.

He had become involved in the drug scene in college, mainly because his roommate was a source for the supply. He was one of those fortunate ones who could occasionally take drugs, usually only marijuana, but never became truly addicted. On a few occasions he had tried cocaine but frankly didn't like the feeling of losing control. There were times when he agreed to do a favor for his roommate and actually deliver some drugs, and on one occasion he picked up drugs from a supplier off campus. He was never comfortable in doing this since he felt it began to cross that invisible line where the risk was too great. Dick had a sort of internal gauge that told him when he was reaching that point.

Allison was truly excited with anticipation, probably more so than at any other time in her life. Today she would be released from the Spaulding Rehabilitation Hospital after months of confinement since her injuries. Her recovery had progressed well, even though the head injury had initially left her with some motor problems, especially on her left side. Over the weeks in rehab, however, she was gradually getting her strength back, and the physicians felt that she eventually would recover almost one hundred percent of the use of her arm and leg.

She would have to be monitored closely at home and spend time at a local physical therapy clinic several times each week for the next few months. Her parents had convinced her to stay with them initially, and she had reluctantly agreed. It had been difficult to give up the independence that she had thrived on since college, but her physician would not have released her from Spaulding if she were going to be at home alone. She at times still had headaches and occasionally felt a little dizzy, but these episodes were becoming less and less frequent.

There had been no further developments regarding the circumstances surrounding her injuries. Amy had contacted the police and found that they had Allison's bike in storage. With Amy's encouragement, Allison agreed to meet with the police even though she could not remember any more details regarding the car that had hit her. Two detectives came to the hospital for the interview and listened to Allison describe the incident and what she had heard and seen, including the color of the car. They had then sent the bike for forensic analysis to see if there was any evidence of it being hit by a car before it struck the tree. Although Allison had emphasized that her recollection was vague, they especially examined the bike for any indication of green paint that might have come from the auto. They also took Allison's clothes that she had been wearing at the time of the accident and sent them for a complete forensic analysis, again with the thought that perhaps there would be some indication of whether she was struck by a car. After a couple of weeks, they had come back to Allison and indicated that there was no evidence of a vehicle having been involved. They spent some time questioning her further to try to elicit more details, but her memory had not recovered anything further. Seemingly this had now become a closed issue in the eyes of the police. Allison questioned herself over and over about the incident, and even though she could not remember any more specifics, she was increasingly convinced that she had been the victim of a hit-and-run accident. For a while she expected that with time she would remember more, but with each passing week she began to realize that there were some parts of the accident that she would probably never recall.

She was anxious to get back to work, but she was told by her physician that it would still be several months before she would be physically able to drive her car, never mind return to her job. The company and her associates had been most understanding about the length of her recovery period, and her supervisor had suggested that when the time was right she might start by working at home for a while. One of the advantages of her job was that much of it could be done away from the office as long as she had a computer to access and download the necessary information.

One thing that truly upset Allison was that the injuries had prevented her from studying for her next actuarial exam. However, even now as she was leaving the rehab hospital, she had to admit to herself that she did not have the energy to concentrate on studying for any extended period of time. She had been assured by her physicians that given time she would have a full recovery with few if any residual effects. The schedule she had put together for completing her studies and being certified as a fellow would probably have to be extended out for at least another year.

Amy had continued to visit her weekly as she continued her recovery. They talked about her coming to Nantucket for several weeks in the summer to stay with Amy and the children while she continued her recuperation. Although that really sounded appealing to Allison, she wasn't at all ready to admit that she would not be able to return to work by that time. Allison had visited Nantucket almost every summer for one or two weeks since she and Amy were in college, and she truly enjoyed the island. It was a time away when she could truly relax without the weekly schedule of work and study.

There were so many things she could look forward to. In the past she had taken frequent bike rides on the many bike paths around the island. There were close to forty miles of these paths that stretched from one end of the island to the other. They were well away from the commercial area of town, and most of them offered beautiful scenery of conservation land, cranberry bogs, small ponds, and the moors. She usually alternated the biking with some early morning jogging on the same bike paths, early enough to avoid the summer crowds.

Although she particularly enjoyed the physical activity, she also looked forward to relaxing and sunning on the beach, especially this year when her injuries would somewhat limit her usual fitness activity. She dreamed about the opportunities to play with Amy's children at Jetties Beach, and she knew they always looked forward to Auntie Al's visit. She looked forward to indulging in a large ice cream cone at the Juice Bar, one with their specially made waffle cones, and regular walks on the beaches would offer opportunities to find some sea glass to add to her collection. *Even though there won't be as much bike riding or jogging this summer, I know that getting away and spending time with the children and Amy will be good for me. It'll give me a chance to gain back my strength and get a little tan. I've been inside so long my skin has never looked so pale.*

April 2009

The island of Nantucket is about twenty-six miles south of Cape Cod and can be reached in several ways. Frequent daily commercial plane schedules from New York, Boston, and Providence had brought the island much closer to metropolitan areas than had been true a quarter century ago, and there were twenty-minute flights on small commuter planes available to and from Hyannis on Cape Cod every hour year round. The auto and truck ferry made several trips each day, again year round, but the travel time was more than two hours, so it was not the preferred way to travel unless you were taking your car. In the mid-nineties "fast ferry" catamaran service had been initiated, for passengers only, and made the crossing in only one hour and, of course, at less cost than flying. In the busy months of July and August, all of the different alternatives for getting to and leaving the island were on many days filled to their capacity.

The easier and more frequent access to the island had resulted in an ever-increasing flow of tourists as well as a vibrant building boom through the early years of the twenty-first century; however, with the advent of the severe economic slowdown and recession in 2008, new construction had come almost to a complete stop. Over the previous twenty-five-year period, automobile traffic had increased and the year-round population had grown to more than ten thousand; however, on a busy weekend in the summer, the population ballooned to more than fifty thousand. Still, because of its physical isolation in the ocean, it still retained much of its charm as a small town that was not subject to the influence of suburban malls, interstate highways, traffic lights, and the other characteristics of twenty-first-century life. This was especially true in the winter when the ferry and flight schedules were scaled back and many seasonal residents and tourists went south to find a warmer climate. Most of the year-round residents relished the solitude of the winter months, a time for reading and socializing with family and friends and generally recovering from the busy hubbub of the summer season.

Along with the growth came an increase in crime on the island, much of it mirroring the types of offenses one would find on the mainland. Significant drug and alcohol problems plagued both the adult and teenage population, and the increase in various kinds of crimes was often linked to drugs. The fact that a high percentage of the homes and cottages on the island were seasonal and vacant during a significant part of the year was, of course, one reason for so many incidents of breaking-and-entering crimes.

Since their marriage, Jack and Amy Kendrick had used the summer home on the island that was owned by Amy's parents, and

Amy and the children spent most of the summer months there, with Jack commuting down from Boston on most weekends. And even during the late spring and early fall they would frequently take a long weekend to get away from the hustle and bustle of city life. The new photography business in Boston, however, had limited the number of weekends Jack was able to make the trip.

This particular weekend in mid-April was Jack's first trip of the new year and therefore the first time to their summer home since they had closed it up the previous October. They had a caretaker who checked the house weekly during the winter and would call them if there were any problems. Jack made the trip alone to open up the house—turn on the water, put out the yard furniture, take out the storm windows and put in the screens, rake and clean up the yard—reversing everything that he'd done to close up the house the previous fall. On this particular visit, everything appeared to be fine from the exterior of the house, and even when walking through the house everything looked as he would expect; even the musty smell from several months of being closed up was a welcome aroma and a sign of summer coming.

After turning on the water and turning up the heat to take the chill out of the house, he began to check through each of the rooms. Nothing looked amiss until he opened the TV cabinet and found that the television, CD player, and the DVD/VCR tape player were all missing. He checked the master bedroom and found that the TV there was also missing.

Out loud he said, "What the hell. Goddamn it, someone has broken in!"

He began to systematically check the other rooms to see if anything else was missing. He immediately thought of Amy's jewelry, but then he remembered that she never left any on the island. Then he thought to himself, *Hell, she doesn't have much of value anyway. As a matter of fact, there isn't much else in the house that anyone would be interested in stealing.*

He was about to call the police when he began to wonder how the person or persons had gotten into the house. He checked the two exterior doors and could not see any evidence that they had been tampered with, and he then checked all of the windows to see if they were locked. Since they all had storm windows pulled down for the winter, there was no way anyone could have entered without breaking a storm window first. All of the windows were intact. He finally checked the cellar door and windows and here again found that nothing was amiss.

Jack was truly puzzled. He placed the call to the police station, gave them the information, and they said they'd have an officer out to the house shortly.

While he waited for the police, he decided not to do any more of his chores in order not to disturb anything that might be of importance. He sat on the living room couch, staring at the open TV cabinet, and became increasingly angry.

Jesus Christ, that was a new flat screen TV, and the DVD and stereo system were only a couple of years old. Just when we're trying to get this new business going we don't need any additional expenses. The TV in the bedroom wasn't worth all that much, but it'll cost something to replace it, not to mention the aggravation and time to buy new ones. Well, maybe the home insurance will pick up part of the cost. I wonder how much of a deductible we have.

The house was only about a mile from the center of town in a residential area and on a small side street off of Madaket Road. Although the wood-shingled homes in the area were built for year-round occupancy, most of them were owned by off-island people, like Jack and Amy, who occupied them mostly in the summer and for a few weekends throughout the fall and spring.

The police detective arrived in less than fifteen minutes. Jack recognized him as one of the detectives who had been involved in the investigation of the murder on the steamship a few years earlier, and in turn the detective recognized Jack as the one who had helped solve the murder. The fact that a terrorist attack had been linked to the murder resulted in tremendous national and international press coverage that swamped the island with more attention than anyone wished for, and it had continued for several weeks. Jack himself had received a lot of publicity, especially surrounding the numerous photos that he had taken of most of the key players in the incident. It was the money from the sale of those photos to various media outlets that had allowed him to open his business in Boston.

Jack described to the detective the items that were missing, and then the detective began to make his own examination of the house. After several minutes he suggested that they sit down and have Jack give him more specific details regarding the items.

"First of all, I have to tell you that we've had a very large number of break-ins over the winter, and several in this area. This one seems pretty typical since whoever is responsible seems to stick to the big-ticket items—TVs, stereos, DVD players. We're pretty sure it's not kids since it appears to be well organized, and there's no evidence of vandalism. Because we have so many vacant houses in isolated areas, we're a big target over the winter months. You may have seen a couple of articles in the *Inquirer and Mirror* talking about the robberies."

Jack shook his head and said, "Yeah, I think I do remember seeing something, but frankly I didn't pay much attention."

"One thing that's different in this instance is that there's no evidence of breaking and entering. Most of the other situations involved a broken window or broken door lock where someone gained entry, but in this case everything looks pretty clean. Usually we get a call from a caretaker reporting the crime because he's seen evidence of the break-in."

"I can't figure that out. We do have a caretaker, but there wouldn't have been any reason for him to open and check out the TV cabinets since there was no evidence of any forced entry."

"Well, one of the things we need to talk about is who else has keys to the house other than the caretaker."

Jack thought for a minute and said, "There really aren't many. We have a cleaning person who comes in periodically during the summer, and we have a babysitter who has a key, but both of them have been working for us for years. I'll double-check with my wife to see if she remembers anyone else."

"How about any construction or service workers you may have given a key to who did work when you were off island? You know, it doesn't have to recent. I sometimes find that people have given keys to various people to do work in their homes but never got the keys back."

"I can't think of anyone, but again let me check with my wife."

"Do you keep a spare key anywhere outside?"

"Yes, we do. I hadn't thought of that. There's one hung in the outside shower stall in the back of the house."

They both got up and went to check the location of the key, and it was still in its place.

Detective Hines said, "Well, the fact that it's still here doesn't mean that it wasn't used. I have to tell you that putting a key in this kind of location is not uncommon, and thieves tend to know where to look. One of the first places is inside sheds, garages, or shower stalls."

Jack just stared and didn't say anything.

"I'll come back later and take some fingerprints around the stall and the TV cabinets, but I don't think it'll lead us anywhere."

"Where do all of these stolen TVs end up?"

"Well, we're pretty sure they're taken off island and sold to some fence. In the past we've arrested a couple of people for receiving stolen property and sent them off to jail, but the large increase in the number of robberies makes us think that we're now dealing with a pretty sophisticated organization that's moving the stolen property off island. I've been spending a lot of my time in the past several weeks chasing down leads and suspects, but I haven't had a break yet."

Hines paused and then said, "I'd like a list of all of the items that were stolen—makes, models, description, and so forth."

"Yeah, I'll try to get all that together for you."

"And get me the list of people who may have duplicates of your keys. We'll run them against other lists we have and see if there are any hits."

"OK, and thanks for coming out so quickly."

Jack called Amy, filled her in on what he'd found, and asked her about who else might have keys. There were a couple of workers who had done jobs in the past, but they were both quite certain that those workers had returned the keys. Jack let his emotion and anger flow over the phone, and Amy tried to reassure him that everything would work out and that it could be a lot worse. It looked like whoever had broken in must have used the key in the shower stall. He thought to himself, *How stupid can I get?*

Jack finally went back to his chores. He had less than two days to complete them as well as try to finalize the rental arrangement he had made to exhibit and sell some of his photography work this summer on the island. He and Amy had decided to open up a small photography shop in the waterfront area and display many of the photographs that Jack had taken over the years on his many trips to the island. Amy was especially excited about the opportunity to expand their business while they were vacationing on the island. There were several art shops in the downtown area, many of them close to the piers where many summer visitors moored their yachts in the summer.

August 2008

Ed Fletcher, sitting at his desk at work on this Thursday morning, called Dick Gimble in the claim department and spoke softly so as not to be overheard by coworkers, but he was obviously upset. "Dick, I've got to see you as soon as possible. Let's go out for lunch."

"What's up?"

Ed hesitated and said, "I really can't say over the phone, but it's important and has to do with our, uhhhhh, project."

Dick, trying to decipher what Ed was talking about, thought for a minute and replied, "Oh, OK. Where do you want to go?"

With a definite tremor in his voice, Ed said, "Why don't you grab a sandwich and soda from the cafeteria and meet me at my car in the parking lot?"

"OK, see you a little after noon."

Dick and Ed were now into their fifth year with their claim fraud scheme, and after starting slowly and somewhat cautiously, they had gradually expanded the scheme so that in the previous year they each had pocketed around fifty thousand dollars—all of it tax free. They had carefully designed the program so that the phony applications were not so large that they would warrant any careful or detailed underwriting investigation. They never submitted more than one application a week, and it became lost in the more than eighty thousand that typically came into the company every year. Ed had worked to design an application profile that would slip through the cracks and he was also in a position to track the applications once they arrived in the company.

Similarly, Dick had designed a profile of the type of claim that would be the least likely to receive scrutiny—accidents rather than sicknesses, and disabilities that lasted no more than four or five weeks. The fraudulent claims were submitted a few weeks after each policy had been approved, so under their scheme there averaged one new claim each week, and no more than four or five were open at any one time since each one averaged about four weeks in duration. As a new claim was opened on a new policy, there was one that had been open for a few weeks that closed. John Adams Insurance had more than half a million disability policyholders insured, and here again the phony claims had been lost among the tens of thousands of legitimate claims. Dick was also in a position where he could follow the claims as they were processed to make certain no unusual investigation was conducted. During the previous five years they had submitted more than two hundred fraudulent claims without any hitches, and with no one raising any questions. They had a foolproof scheme.

Even though the system had been working flawlessly since 2004, Ed continued to be extremely anxious about getting caught. By nature he was a worrier and did not possess a great deal of self-confidence, and certainly he was not the natural risk taker that Dick was. Initially, he resisted Dick's pressure to enter into the scheme, and he agreed only when Dick suggested they "try a few more" to see if the experiment really would work. After a few weeks they each had been able to pocket more than four thousand dollars, and Ed saw that his personal money problems were easing. He was even able to pay down some of his credit card debt. As the scheme expanded, always at Dick's insistence, Ed simply never refused to go along. As the weeks turned to months, he became hooked, similar to the person who tries drugs socially but then gets hooked and addicted. He would frequently express his anxiety, usually by saying either, "I'm really uncomfortable," or "What if we get caught?" Dick would assure him that the scheme was truly foolproof, and as each month and year went by, it became more logical to assume that he was right, not to mention the fact that each of them became more and more dependent on the extra income.

However, on this particular day Ed was convinced that his fears were finally proving to be right. He met Dick in the parking lot, and they drove to a small lake close by where they could park the car. Ed had begun to excitedly explain his fears.

"Dick, they know all about our phony claims."

"What are you talking about?"

Ed spoke with increased anxiety. "The actuarial department. They've been running some studies and have discovered what we're doing. Dick, they're going to catch us. Jesus, we're going to end up in jail. I kept telling you that it was too risky."

"Ed, for Christ's sake, will you keep calm and slow down and tell me exactly what's happening?"

"I heard this morning that the actuaries have found some unusual results in their claim studies for last year. They said that they've seen an increase in the company's accident claims, especially in the early policy years. Jesus, Dick, that's us!"

"Is that all you've heard?"

"Yeah, but for God's sake, that's enough. What are we going to do?"

Dick thought for a minute and then said, "Well, for right now we're not going to change anything. Don't panic. You know every year the actuaries run all kinds of studies, and this probably has nothing at all to do with our claims. Think about it for minute. Our claims are only a drop in the bucket—a few thousand dollars in comparison to several million. Let's just cool it while I try to get a little more information."

"I don't know. I think we've been had."

"Who did you hear this from?"

"I was getting a cup of coffee this morning and overheard a couple of actuaries talking."

"Who were they?"

"Well, one was this girl, Allison something or other, who handles the disability line in actuarial, and the other one I don't know. I've seen him around before, but I don't know his name."

"What else did they say?"

"Well, this girl Allison said she'd stumbled on it while doing her regular annual review of disability claims, and even though it wasn't a big dollar amount, it showed an unusual trend from previous years. She specifically talked about accident claims in their early years' and that the frequency of them was way out of proportion to what they should be. She did say she didn't know when she'd be able to dig into it further because she had some other studies that her boss wanted her to complete."

"Sounds to me like this isn't a priority and isn't as big a problem in her mind as you think it is. If it's anything to do with our claims, it just may blow over anyway."

Ed hesitated and replied sort of in resignation, "I don't know."

Dick was truly more concerned than he let on. The fact that the actuary was talking about accident claims was getting too close to their situation. He looked at Ed, conscious of how jittery he was, and said, "OK, Ed, I really don't think there's anything to this, but let's be cautious and back off with any new applications or new claims while we try to find out more. You keep your ears open and let me know if you hear anything more. In the meantime, I'll do some poking around on my own and see what I can find out."

"Yeah, but I have to tell you I'm scared to hell."

"Let's not panic yet."

May 2009

Allison had been at her parents' home for about two months recuperating. Her residual injuries from the accident were steadily improving, and more importantly, her energy and enthusiasm were returning. She was anxious to get back to her regular routines—work, study, and exercise—but she knew that she was not quite ready. Her physician had cautioned her several weeks ago to go slow and focus her energy on her rehabilitation program, and she had to admit his advice seemed to be paying off.

Amy had encouraged her to spend a month on Nantucket beginning in early July, and she was looking forward to that change in scenery and especially getting away from her mother's constant doting over her. It had been years since she had spent so much time with her parents, and she found that the old saying "one never stops parenting" was true. It would be good to see Amy and Jack's children, smell some fresh ocean air, sit on the beach, soak up some sun, and begin her bike riding again.

During the last few weeks she had found that her level of concentration had improved considerably, and she was able to spend longer periods of time at the computer without becoming tired or experiencing a headache. She had talked with her boss, Bill Alberti, at JAIC, and he had agreed to let her spend time continuing her analysis of claim experience for the previous year. It was routine and necessary for the actuarial department to spend considerable time each year examining the claim trends from previous years to ascertain whether the actual experience was consistent with the assumptions they had made in setting the premium rates. When they were able to establish consistent and significant trends, either favorable or unfavorable, then it was necessary to determine what was causing the claim experience to be different from what had been assumed in setting the premium rates. Changes in the claim results could be caused by a variety of things, such as improvements in medical treatments that shortened the length of disabilities, recessions that tended to increase the length of time people remained disabled, poor underwriting quality, or lax claim investigation. The actuary needed to determine what was causing the variance and then decide whether some adjustment needed to be made in the rates, underwriting procedures, claim procedures, or product design. One of the important determinations was whether or not the trend was a permanent or temporary one.

Allison had been studying claim costs and trends for three years and had developed an understanding and sense for when things didn't appear quite right. One of the abnormalities she had noticed when she was studying the disability claim experience before she was injured was an increase in the number of accident claims over the previous three years. Although the total cost of these claims was not large in comparison to all of the disability claims, the fact that there was an increasing trend in the number of them had caused her to investigate further. She had begun to develop a profile of the nature of these claims—the kind of injury, age, occupation, and sex of claimants, length of the disability, amount of the claim, geographic location—and she continued to look for any other similarities.

Before she was injured, she had come to believe that the adverse trend was not an aberration, and she had discovered that there appeared to be some common characteristics with many of the claims. They were all small policies, they were relatively new policies, many of the claims seemed to last only about four or five weeks, and the policies had subsequently all lapsed for nonpayment of the premium shortly after the claim was closed. There were no long-term or permanent disability claims in the group, and that in itself was strange when looking at the large number of claims she had accumulated. Finally, by far the majority of these claims were in the northeast region of the country.

She had discussed the findings with her boss a few weeks before her injury, and although he was interested, he indicated that since the total cost of the variance was not very large, he'd rather have her focus on other studies where there were more substantial deviations. He suggested that she should work on this accident claim study only in her spare time. She had to somewhat agree since there were always other projects or studies that were pressing; however, she was still intrigued by the trends and was concerned that if they continued, then the financial implications might truly become significant.

She had subsequently found time at home over a few weekends to do some further evaluation of the problem, and she became more and more convinced that something unusual was occurring that she couldn't put her finger on. She could find no similar trends in other geographic areas of the country where the occupations, ages, type of injuries, and sizes of policies were occurring in such large numbers. It just didn't make sense that all of these variances could be centered in one geographic area. It also didn't make sense that a policyholder would allow his or her policy to lapse immediately after receiving a sizeable claim payment. Usually a policyholder who had benefited from a claim payment was most likely to keep the policy and pay the premiums. And so, one of the first projects that Allison wanted to dig into during her recovery was to try to further determine what was causing the increase in accident claims in the northeast part of the country.

She figured that her boss's agreement to let her work on her accident study might be to sort of let her gradually get back into things without being involved in something that was particularly critical to the company. That was OK with her, and as a matter of fact, during her recovery the past few months, it was this unresolved claim study she had most frequently thought about. Her nature had always been one where any unsolved riddle or puzzle gnawed at her until she figured out the answer.

May 2009

Amy Kendrick truly enjoyed her life as a stay-at-home mom, especially now when the children were a little older and didn't require as much personal attention. Jeremy was now in first grade, and Natalie, a four-year-old, spent three mornings each week at pre-school. She had thought about substitute teaching when Jack first opened his photography business in order to help out financially as they tried to get the new venture going profitably. Although they had the hundred thousand dollars from the sale of Jack's photographs of the terrorist attack, they knew that any start-up business was a risk.

However, the Boston business had caught on immediately, and their first year sales were half again as much as they had planned.

Amy was an excellent manager of the financial end of the business and was always careful they didn't overspend on some of their supplies and equipment. She'd located wholesale suppliers for framing and for other photography materials that allowed them to have a good margin on the final products they sold. Jack, being the artist, was inclined to sometimes go overboard on the type and style of framing materials he thought he needed for a particular photograph. Amy would frequently remind him that he had to keep the cost at a level that would be attractive to the buyer while still having a decent profit for the business. Together they proved to be sound business partners as well as having a sound marriage.

A few months previously, Amy had suggested to Jack that they open another photo shop on Nantucket during the summer months. He had a portfolio of dozens of scenes on the island that he had taken over the years, and they had sold very well at the Boston store. She was certain that they would sell at least as well on the island because of the large number of visitors in the summer, and she was going to be on the island anyway. She thought they could find someone to help run the shop for some of the hours each day since she would be busy much of the time caring for the children; however, she would still find time to manage and supervise the operation.

There were numerous art studios on the island, but they still felt there was a place for Jack's kind of photography. She knew from experience that the quality of his work was appreciated and becoming well recognized, and there had even been an article in the *Boston Globe* last year highlighting Jack's business and its success. He had become sort of a local hero, both in Boston and Nantucket, because of the role he played in the capture of those involved in the terrorist attack. Having some local notoriety certainly didn't hurt his business prospects.

On this weekend in late May, Amy and Jack had come to the island to finalize the arrangements for the photo shop. They had been cautious about moving ahead too quickly and overextending themselves financially, especially considering the cost of renting space and the natural financial risk of expanding the business. One of Amy's friends, Kathy Abraham, was a local artist who sold her paintings in a few shops during recent summers but was also reluctant to open up her own business. However, over the winter they had explored the thought of opening up the shop jointly and offering customers a choice of both kinds of artwork, paintings and photography.

They had located some available space for a small shop on one of the piers in the boat basin. During the summer months the number of pleasure boats, both motor and sail, numbered in the hundreds, and many of them were large yachts, some exceeding one hundred feet in length. There were sailing races for every class of boat over the summer, and almost every weekend from late Memorial Day to early September there was some racing event that attracted many sailors from the mainland. It was not unusual for boats to appear that were registered in Bermuda and the Caribbean islands and occasionally even from Europe. There were also a few races that were well known by yachtsmen up and down the east coast that drew some of the America's Cup class of boats and offered a true spectacle for the onlookers. Jack had taken several pictures over the years of some of the well-known boats that had raced in America's Cup races in the past.

The "boat people" were excellent potential customers for the shop, and the location of the shop enhanced the possibility of success. In addition, the boat basin with the hundreds of different styles and sizes of boats was a favorite place for tourists and townspeople to stroll around taking in a lifestyle that many only dreamed about. Part of their strolling included visiting the various shops along the wharfs, and many of the tourists were looking for a memento to remember their visit.

The cost of renting the shop for the three-month season would have been too much for either Amy or Kathy alone, but together they felt it was something that was doable. They had spent the weekend deciding how they would display their artwork, how many framed paintings and photographs could be placed on the walls, working out a schedule for staffing the shop, and deciding what other display materials they both would need. They also finalized arrangements with a local teacher who would manage the shop when neither Amy nor Kathy was available.

As they left the island on Sunday to return to their home in Quincy, Amy was truly excited and looking forward to the summer. She had always enthusiastically anticipated spending time on the island since she was a child and made the annual trip with her parents. During the last few years she had enjoyed seeing the same excitement in her children that she remembered as a child. Both Jeremy and Natalie had become true water rats, and Amy spent much of her summer days at one of the many beaches.

They had purchased new televisions, a CD player, and a DVD/VCR tape player to replace those that had been stolen, and thankfully their home insurance had covered much of the cost. During the visit they realized that a few more items were missing, including a mantel clock and a common print of an island scene, and Jack had called the police to update the list of stolen items.

In addition to the excitement of this new business venture, Amy also looked forward to spending time with Allison Sheppard when she came to the island to continue her recuperation. She had seen Allison improve steadily over the past several months and could appreciate her impatience about being able to resume her normal lifestyle. Allison had expressed her frustration at living at home with her parents, and Amy was certain that the more relaxed lifestyle on the island would help speed her recuperation. When the two of them had gotten together in recent years, the time had always passed by too quickly as they reminisced about past experiences and brought each other up to date on current events; this summer would give them an opportunity to truly reinvigorate their friendship.

May 2009

Al Collins, the senior detective on the Nantucket police force, was under some significant pressure from the chief to solve the substantial increase in the breaking and entering crimes that occurred over the winter and spring. The chief let him know in no uncertain terms that he was constantly being questioned by not only the town manager and the board of selectmen, but he was increasingly hearing from the general public. Both of the weekly newspapers had run several articles over the past few months on the increase in crime, and more recently editorials had appeared inquiring as to what the police department was doing to solve the problem. There were even strongly worded suggestions that perhaps they needed some new blood in the department and that some of the police staff were too provincial and didn't have the experience necessary to handle this sort of increasing crime wave. Al had bristled when he first read the article. *What the hell do they know about it anyway? I'm working my ass off trying to get to the bottom of this. I don't have enough staff to follow all the leads, and for God's sake, we're not talking about a murder.*

Al had grown up on the island and had worked in the police department for some fifteen years since returning from a four-year stint in the army, where he had been assigned to the military police. When he was discharged, it was logical for him to secure a job with the local police, and from the beginning he had considered it a long-term career. He was very ambitious and to others always seemed too anxious to find opportunities to advance his position, often at the expense of others. He had been the detective assigned to investigate the death of a federal Drug Enforcement Administration official on the island a few years earlier, and although he had little to do with finally solving the case, he had found every opportunity to take the credit.

Al was well known to most everyone on the island, was a physically imposing individual, and had been a better-than-average athlete in high school. He carried himself with an air of overconfidence that was clearly evident to others, but his outgoing and gregarious nature had a way of defusing what otherwise might have been an objectionable personality. Those who worked closely with him, however, were always somewhat cautious in their personal dealings. They had experienced too many situations where he had taken some information and used it to his own advantage.

Jack Kendrick had dealt with Collins a few years previously during the drug investigation that had finally become entangled with the terrorist attack in Boston. Jack recalled well his dealings with Collins during that time, and he also remembered the fact that Al had at one point believed that Jack himself was in some way involved in the drug ring. It had been an extremely difficult time for Jack and Amy, and Jack had finally conducted his own investigation into the events and cleared his name, resulting in his both solving the terrorist attack and breaking up the drug ring. Although everything eventually turned out OK, Jack had had enough personal contact with Collins that he was apprehensive about any further involvement.

In spite of this reluctance, Jack called Collins, since he knew that he was the one in charge of the investigation into the wave of break-ins on the island, and he wanted to inquire about the investigation into the robbery at his summer home.

Al was his typical outgoing self in his telephone conversation with Jack, but below the surface his frustration grew over what he perceived as still another public complaint about the unsolved wave of crime. He had the capacity to exclude from his memory those experiences or incidents that showed his own personal weaknesses or shortcomings, and so he had no concerns, misgivings, or regrets about the fact that he had wrongly suspected and indeed accused Jack of being involved the drug ring. His entire focus was on the adverse publicity with his current investigation and what effect it would have on his career.

Jack said, "Detective Collins, this is Jack Kendrick. You remember me from the drug and terrorist incident a couple of years ago?"

"Oh hi, Jack. Sure I remember. How have you been?"

"I'm pretty well. I'm calling about the robbery I had at our summer home over the winter. I met with your Detective Hines when I was down here several weeks ago, and I wonder if you've had any luck in your investigation."

Al thought to himself that he'd like to say, *I might have a chance of solving it if people like you would stop hassling me so I'd have time to follow up on some of the leads.*

However, he said in his controlled manner, "Yeah, I knew you'd had a break-in, and I don't have anything to tell you right now. You probably know that we've had a rash of them over the winter, and we're working as hard as we can, chasing down every possible lead."

"Well, my wife and I are down here this weekend, and I thought I'd call to see if there had been any developments or if there's any more information you need from me."

"No, I think we have everything we need—unless you've thought of something else or you've found some other things missing."

Jack replied, "No, we haven't found anything else missing, but I'll certainly let you or Detective Hines know if we notice anything."

"OK, Jack, and we'll be sure to let you know if anything develops."

Al hung up the phone without really waiting for Jack's response. *These damn summer people think the world revolves around them. They've got more money than they know what to do with, and the loss of this guy's TV probably didn't even put a dent in his pocketbook.*

He had a meeting scheduled with the chief later in the day, and Al knew that the chief wanted to bring in the state police to play a bigger role in the investigation. Al's ego wouldn't allow him to admit that he could use someone else's eyes and resources in helping to solve what had become a very public problem, so his primary preparation for the meeting focused on how he could continue to maintain control.

September 2008

Dick Gimble had asked Ed Fletcher over to his apartment on this Sunday evening to discuss further what they'd learned about the actuarial investigations of the claim results that Ed was convinced had uncovered their fraud scheme.

When Ed arrived, Dick noticed that he was nervous, even exhibiting a small tremor in his hands. Dick got a beer for each of them, and they sat down in his cramped sitting area. It was three weeks after Ed had overheard the conversation between the two actuaries, a conversation that had resulted in several sleepless nights since their last discussion. Dick, on the other hand, appeared relaxed, even though he too had become increasingly concerned that Ed's suspicions may have been well founded.

"OK, Ed, what more have you found out?"

"Nothing really, but I still think they're on to us. I've tried a couple of times at lunch to sit close to the same actuaries, but the subject never was mentioned. I've tried to inquire around with some others to see if they've heard anything, but..."

"What are you talking about? You haven't mentioned it to anyone else, have you?"

"No, no, I've been really careful when I ask questions. I've simply casually asked a couple of underwriters if they'd heard anything about last year's claim results. We all know that the actuaries always examine claim experience for the previous year, and not infrequently we'll get a memo to watch out for certain things that they see as possible problems. You know, sometimes as a result of their studies we'll actually change our underwriting rules as to when and what we investigate."

"Well, I hope you really were careful. If you appear too interested, it may come back to haunt us."

"Have you heard anything?"

Dick hesitated before continuing. "Well, nothing much more than we know already."

"What do you mean 'much more'?"

Dick had done some checking on his own and had turned up some information that confirmed what Ed had heard previously. He had a friend in the actuarial department who was always anxious to point out to others how important the actuaries were in making certain the other departments were doing their jobs properly. His demeanor of self-importance frequently resulted in his talking quite freely. Dick had asked the actuary what they were working on, and after a while Dick brought the conversation around to inquiring casually about Allison Sheppard and what she was working on. The actuary had kidded Dick about having a romantic interest in Allison, but Dick had carefully assured him that he knew Allison had recently been assigned to the disability area and that he didn't know her. Since he was involved with disability claims, he said he had a natural interest in who was assigned to that product line in the actuarial department. His friend had offered to introduce him to Allison, and Dick had agreed. A few days later when Dick went to the cafeteria for lunch, his friend was sitting at a table with Allison and invited Dick to join them.

After some casual conversation, Dick had expressed interest in Allison's new job and asked what she was working on. Demonstrating her natural shyness, she had replied that, among other things, she was in the middle of the annual claim analysis of the previous year. He expressed interest and asked her what she had learned. During the conversation she said, "Well sort of by accident I've stumbled across some interesting trends in accident claims that don't make a lot of sense."

She went on to explain the increase in the number of accident claims and asked him if he had noticed anything unusual in his claim handling. He quickly replied that he hadn't seen anything out of the ordinary and inquired about what her next steps were. She told him that the study was not a high priority for her manager because the total dollar amount was not especially large, but she emphasized that she was still intrigued. She mentioned that she had been pursuing her investigation further on her own time and had noticed a few other things, such as the fact that the claims were all on recently issued polices and that the policies lapsed shortly after the claims ended. She finally sort of shrugged it off by saying it was probably just an aberration, but that it bothered her not to be able to come up with a logical explanation. He especially remembered her finally saying, "I hate to walk away from something without an answer. It drives me crazy not to know what's really behind the adverse claim numbers."

Dick would have liked to pursue the conversation further but felt he might be crossing a line and appear too interested. He had simply ended the conversation by emphasizing the fact that it probably was an aberration.

The luncheon conversation had continued to bother him, especially the fact that she was continuing her investigation on her own time. If she went further, she might begin to tie in some other facts, such as the premium payment scheme that would be identical on all the policies and might eventually be tied back to them.

Ed asked again, clearly impatient, "What do you mean 'much more'?"

Dick had decided not to tell Ed all of the details of the conversation with Allison because he was fearful of how Ed would react when he learned that Allison's investigation had clearly stumbled on their scheme, and so he replied, "Well, I had a chance to meet the actuary who's doing these studies."

"Jesus, how did you pull that off? What did you find out?"

"Well, you know she's only been in the disability area for about a year, and she said she just sort of stumbled on the accident claim problem. She didn't seem to put a lot of credence in its importance because the total amounts were small in comparison to the total claims. I don't think we have anything to worry about."

"Are you sure about that?"

Continuing to downplay his own fears, Dick said, "Yeah, I really don't think this is going anywhere."

"Well, I hope you're right, but I really don't feel any more relaxed, and I don't think we should continue on with the project."

"Yeah, I think that's the right thing for now, but we're both going to find ourselves strapped for cash. Maybe we can tweak the program a little and avoid the areas she's looking at."

"Dick, I don't want to be involved any further."

"Look, let's not jump to conclusions too quickly. We should both keep our ears to the ground to see if anything further develops. I really think there's a good chance it'll just blow over."

October 2008

Dick Gimble had experienced several sleepless nights since the luncheon with Allison Sheppard when he found out more details about her claim investigation. He figured that he was facing two problems. First, the possibility that she would dig further into the accident claims and find a trail that led to him and Ed. He thought their method of how they paid the premium was the weakest spot in their scheme since they used the same bank account number over and over, even though in each case it was an electronic transaction with a fictitious name. Still, if someone dug deep enough, they might be able to trace it back to them through the bank. Even more important was the fact that if Allison were to look at the claim files further, she might notice his name would show up as the claim examiner on most of the claims.

The second problem was that the loss of the additional money he had been getting from the fraudulent claims was truly putting him in a hole financially. He had come to depend on the regular extra dollars that had amounted to some fifty thousand dollars, tax free, for both him and Ed in the past twelve months. He had bought a new car and some new furniture for his apartment, but he still had to deal with the alimony and child support payments each month. He had even planned to take a winter vacation in Florida after the first of the year, but that was clearly not going to happen now. He knew he was facing a financial crisis if he didn't do something to solve the money problem.

He remembered that five years previously, when he had first made the bet with Ed that he could pull off the phony claim scheme, he had initially used a different approach. Rather than submit a phony new application, he had taken a recently lapsed policy, paid the premium to reinstate it, and then submitted the claim. They had decided not to use this as their primary scheme since they thought that a large number of quick claims on several policies that had only recently lapsed might be a red flag to claim examiners. However, he figured that he could get away with using this method for a few months now, especially if he made sure that he personally handled all the claims. He could do this without Ed's involvement, and he hoped that after a few months they could perhaps go back to their old scheme.

The more important concern was what Allison might find if she continued her investigation even further. She seemed to be doggedly determined to find a logical reason for the abnormal results and was even pursuing it on her own time. A couple of weeks after their initial lunch, Dick found Allison sitting alone in the cafeteria one noon hour and asked if he could join her. He decided to keep the conversation casual and inquired about where Allison lived and where she had gone to school. He asked how she liked being an actuary and how far along she was in passing her exams to become certified as a fellow. He found out she was an avid biker and had a regular routine of putting in several miles each week. Toward the end of the lunch, he decided to take a risk and casually inquired about the accident claim study.

She replied, "Well, I haven't had much time to do anything further, but every time I look at the data I'm more and more convinced that it's not an aberration. I'm pretty sure it's a fraud scheme of some kind, and even though it may not be millions of dollars, I think it's worth looking into."

Shortly after Allison made this comment they parted, and the subsequent alarm bells in Dick's mind kept him from concentrating on his work for the rest of the day.

October 2008

The town of Upton was close to thirty miles from the John Adams office, and Dick drove out one night after work to see exactly where Allison lived. As he was nearing her apartment, he saw her leaving on her bike, dressed in her workout clothing. As he watched her pick up speed, it was obvious to him that she was a serious biker, and this was her way of getting exercise and staying in shape. The sedentary work life of the John Adams employees meant that many of them, at least those less than fifty years of age, had some serious personal program for keeping fit. He decided not to follow her on this evening but sat in his car for a while mulling over the problems that Allison was causing for him.

The next week he drove out to Upton again and waited in his car several houses away from Allison's apartment until she again appeared with her bike and took off in the same direction. He had learned from his friend in the actuarial department that Allison had a regular routine, three days a week, for her biking and was very deliberate about getting home early enough to be able to get in her exercise before sunset. This particular evening Dick had decided to follow her, and although she rode at a brisk pace for a biker, he found that he had to drive unusually slow to remain inconspicuous. When she entered the state park, he decided that to continue to follow would be too obvious since there were very few cars on the road. As he drove back toward his apartment, he began to formulate a plan, one that would cause him to commit a violent act—something he had never considered or engaged in at any time in his life. But he was desperate.

Two days later he again drove out to Upton and went directly to the state park. He had come early and had driven around for several minutes to identify where there were open stretches on the road and where he might park unobserved. After finalizing the details of a plan in his mind, he parked and waited for Allison to appear. Several times during the past two days he had considered abandoning his plan, but when the time arrived, he found the need to solve his financial crisis was overpowering. As he sat waiting, he noticed there were very few cars driving through the park, and only an occasional biker. Even so he would have to be careful not to be seen by anyone coming in either direction.

He was extremely nervous, his hands perspiring—very unusual for him. Finally he saw Allison appear through his rearview mirror. Although he had pulled off the road to avoid being easily seen, he still slouched down in his seat as she passed. He waited for a full minute to see if any other vehicles or bikes were close by, and then he started his car and quickly sped up to catch Allison. As he rounded a bend, he saw her bike ahead and immediately increased his speed, perspiration now dripping from his forehead. Just before he reached Allison, he looked again in his rearview mirror to make certain no one was behind him and glanced ahead to make certain no cars were coming toward him. As he came abreast of her bike, he cut the wheel sharply to the right and struck her bike, sending her off the road and into the thickly covered woods.

He slowed down for a moment to look out the rearview mirror and saw that she had collided violently with a tree. He then sharply increased his speed to get away from the scene as quickly as possible.

He thought to himself, *How seriously is she injured? Could I have killed her? I really only wanted to complicate her life enough that she'd stop pursuing this investigation. What if she can identify my car? Shit, what have I done? But goddamn it, I didn't have any choice.*

When he arrived back at his apartment, he was visibly shaking and poured himself a stiff drink of bourbon, followed by a second and a third until his mind was dulled to the point of not really caring about what he had just done.

May 2009

Tony Andrews had owned the secondhand store on Nantucket for some fifteen years. He had started out collecting used furniture and a variety of household items at yard sales and then reselling them, a way of picking up a few extra dollars. After a few years, he found that his business had grown to the point where he decided to take the financial plunge and make it his full-time job. He lived in mid island and had inherited the land, a house, and a small barn from his father, whose family had operated a small farm since the mid-1800s.

Tony had accumulated a large assortment of items over the months and years, and the barn proved to be an excellent place to operate his business. There was no other business in town that competed directly with him since most of his customers tended to be those local year-round residents who couldn't afford the high prices one found closer in town at antique shops and the weekend auctions. Those businesses catered mostly to the wealthy summer residents and visitors who could afford to lay down several thousand dollars to furnish their summer homes with used pieces, sometimes antiques, that frequently sold for five and sometimes ten times as much as the proprietor had paid for the item. A Nantucket identity or flavor dramatically increased the price of any item.

Tony over the years had tried many different jobs and was always looking for a way to make a fast buck. In high school he had developed more than a casual use of marijuana and experimented with other drugs, costing him several hundred dollars each month. He had gone to a small local college on the mainland for two years, but he had flunked out and never had a desire to return. He had been arrested while driving under the influence of drugs, but he had been given a suspended sentence since he had no other record. This incident sufficiently scared him that he was able to quit the drug habit, but he had still kept in touch with his friends who were involved in the local drug scene, a growing problem on the island. He knew how to get his hands on drugs, and during those two years in college he had even picked up some serious spare money by supplying drugs to a few close classmates. At that time he had kept his drug dealing to a minimum; he simply was not comfortable with the risk. His supplier at that time was a local friend, a childhood buddy, who ultimately became one of the major dealers on the island. Several years after Tony's failed attempt at college, his friend had finally been caught by the local police, was tried and convicted, and was serving a lengthy state prison sentence at Walpole.

In spite of the risk, Tony saw an opportunity to pick up some real money, and he felt his secondhand business offered some protection that his friend didn't have. He knew the drug crowd well, knew the suppliers on the mainland, was convinced he was much smarter than his friend, and was able to slip into the business easily. His secondhand business had grown briskly, and he had a steady flow of customers. Since most of his island customers worked full time, he kept the business open into the evening and on weekends since this was the time when they were available to shop. This schedule also fit in nicely with the demand for his drug trade, and here again, this part of the business had grown exponentially in the two years since his friend had been incarcerated. He continued to be somewhat apprehensive and aware of the risks but convinced himself that he was careful enough to avoid any trouble, especially with the cover of the legitimate secondhand business.

One of the serious problems, not to mention the risk, of the drug trade was getting his customers to come up with the money to make their habitual purchases. Not long after he began the dealing he found an increasing number of the buyers would bring him items to trade for the drugs. He really didn't mind this kind of transaction since he was able to turn around and sell the items in the regular course of his business. He never asked where the items came from; however, as this method of paying for the drugs grew, he knew that most of it must have been stolen property.

He also became concerned that someone would come in and recognize personal property that had been stolen. Also, by far the largest number of items were televisions, stereos, and DVD players, and he frankly was receiving more of these items than he could reasonably sell on the island, not to mention the fear that these large-ticket items increased the odds that he would get caught.

The solution was logical enough for him. Routinely, about every two weeks, he went off island with his truck to pick up new items for his secondhand business. It was easy for him to load the truck with any items that he couldn't sell on the island or that he felt had a high risk and sell them on the mainland to several secondhand dealers he did business with. The only problem was that it took a whole day away from his business to make the round trip. He had to get up at five o'clock in the morning to get the six thirty vehicle ferry to the mainland, and the crossing took more than two hours each way. He then had to navigate through the sometimes busy Cape Cod traffic to the larger secondhand stores in New Bedford and Brockton, negotiate a price for his items, pick out the items he wanted to buy in return, and then get back to Hyannis for the same two-hour trip back to the island. In addition, there were always some things he needed to buy for his personal use that were either not available on Nantucket or could be found only at a much higher price on the island. It was common for island residents to load up their cars with everything possible, from paper towels and toilet paper to all kinds of groceries, before making the return trip. The premium many merchants on the island demanded for their products was frequently unreasonably high, even taking into consideration that everything had to be transported by ferry. Every stop that Tony made along the way, especially maneuvering his truck in and out of parking lots, took more chunks of time out of his limited schedule.

During the summer months, the ferry made six round trips each day; however, after the summer season ended, the number dropped to three. He frequently found that the last boat that left Hyannis at eight fifteen in the evening was the only one he could comfortably make, especially since one of his additional stops took him out of the way to the dealer who supplied the drugs for his growing list of customers.

He had found this routine worked satisfactorily and reduced the risk to him; consequently, the drug users increasingly bartered their stolen property for their drugs. However, at this point in time Tony was also getting concerned about all of the negative press coverage the increased number of break-ins over the winter was receiving. He was fearful that if one of his drug customers was caught, then the police would quickly be led to his door. He had become extra careful about the stolen items he kept for sale, and he thought he could always claim he didn't know the property was stolen. He also tried to be careful about whom he dealt with. If the drug buyer was someone he didn't know or someone with a bad reputation in the community, he simply refused to do business.

All in all, in spite of the risks, life was good for Tony. His business was earning him a mid-six-figure income, and most of it he couldn't and didn't report on his taxes. He worked hard, putting in many hours, a necessity in this business. He didn't want to bring others into the scheme.

Jack and Amy's stolen electronic equipment showed up at Tony's business, had been shipped off island within a week, and was sold to a secondhand dealer on the mainland. Tony had kept a couple of items he felt could be exhibited for sale in his store without a risk of being discovered as stolen property. One was a mantle clock, not terribly valuable and a common make. Another was a reproduction of a painting of the Nantucket harbor, one where dozens of copies had been made. They were displayed in Tony's shop along with a large number of insignificant items that one frequently finds in secondhand stores.

July 2009

Allison sat by a window as the Hy-Line fast ferry made its way across Nantucket Sound. It seemed to her that for the first time in several months she finally had some time to herself—to take in and truly enjoy the calm ocean surroundings and think ahead about her future. As she looked out the window, every several miles she could pick out a sailboat or a motorized yacht on the horizon either heading for or returning from Nantucket. There were also some small commercial fishing boats that appeared with less frequency, each trying to survive in an industry that had become more and more difficult in Nantucket Sound. She had always coveted her solitude, but the months in the hospital and rehab facility, followed by several months recuperating at her parents' house, left only occasional moments when she was truly alone and could fully relax and enjoy her surroundings.

For the past several weeks she had been looking forward to spending the month in Nantucket with Amy and her family. Even though the house would be active and busy with two young children, she knew that she would find plenty of opportunity to get out and walk on the beach or the moors. Although she hadn't attempted to ride a bike since the accident, she planned on taking advantage of the many bike paths on the island, another opportunity to be alone while at the same time continuing to gain back her physical strength. For the first time since the accident she truly felt that her full recovery was just around the corner.

She had last visited her doctors a week ago and was encouraged by their optimism about her steady progress and future prognosis. The broken leg and dislocated shoulder had completely healed, but she was aware that there was still much work to do to gain back her muscle strength and the range of motion in her shoulder. The extensive physical therapy she had received at the rehabilitation hospital and then the continued twice-a-week therapy while at her parents' had accomplished much in improving her physical condition, but she was frustrated that she was not improving more quickly.

Her doctors remained concerned about her recurring headaches and the fact that she was still unable to fully concentrate for an extended period of time, especially when she was reading a technical document or studying actuarial data. This was her profession, and there had been times when she was fearful that she wouldn't be able to return to the same level of activity that she had always enjoyed. She had tried to study the actuarial material for the next exam that she hoped she would be able to take in the fall; however, after an hour of study she found she simply could not continue. Her physicians continued to reassure her that she was making excellent progress and that she shouldn't be frustrated or concerned. Her head injury and coma had been severe, and it was normal in such situations for there to be lingering residuals—over time they would disappear. Still, Allison was anxious to return to work, to her normal schedule, and to get back to her bike riding.

Because of the head injury she had been advised not to drive her car except for short distances in the local area. The principal problem she had when she first got behind the wheel was the stiffness and decreased mobility in her shoulder. Her sight and concentration while driving had not been a problem at all. During the two months with her parents she had gradually extended the distance she drove, but on this trip to Hyannis on Cape Cod to catch the ferry she chose to travel by bus. She was not yet confident enough to face the possibility of the heavy summer Cape traffic either going or returning from her visit with Amy.

She hoped that after a month relaxing on the island she would be ready to return to her actuarial job at JAIC in August, or at the latest September. She had moved all her belongings from her parents' house back to her apartment a month before she left for Nantucket, and she was truly enjoying being on her own once again. It had been such a long recovery period, and for a young person with Allison's energy and active life it was like being caged. As her strength continued to return and increase, her anxiety to get back to normal began to intensify.

The fast ferry ride on the catamaran was relatively smooth on this day, and the visibility across Nantucket Sound was as clear as one could hope for. After leaving the Hyannis harbor, the catamaran ferry rose up out of the water and quickly reached its cruising speed of about forty knots. The twenty-six-mile crossing took exactly one hour; it was more than twice as fast as the slower auto and truck ferry. Allison recalled one crossing she had made a few years earlier when, returning from a visit with Amy, the ride was truly uncomfortable and, to someone not used to the vagaries of weather and rough seas, downright frightening.

Shortly after the halfway point in the crossing, Allison began looking for the Great Point Lighthouse. It was located on the northeast corner of the island, the closest point to the mainland. The lighthouse could be reached only by four-wheel-drive vehicles, a ride over the sand of some four miles from the point where the roads stopped. During the summer it was a popular excursion for tourists, and not infrequently some inexperienced visitor would get stuck in the sand and the local tow truck operators would earn a hefty fee for pulling the person out. This sandy peninsula was called Coatue and was a protected area for wildlife, especially birds. During much of the year one could find seals sunning themselves under the watchful eye of the lighthouse or simply bobbing their heads in curiosity at the many tourists trying to capture a photo before the seals dove again beneath the waves.

Allison recalled her many past trips out to Coatue as she spotted the lighthouse truly sparkling from the reflection of the sun. She especially remembered going out for a picnic a few years ago with Amy's family one evening and the excitement of the children when Jack caught a bluefish by casting out into the waves off the point below the lighthouse. In the early morning and in the evening one could find several vehicles, many of them pickup trucks, parked at the edge of the sand beyond the lighthouse and the occupants all standing and casting into the ocean hoping to catch bluefish. There was a sandbar extending out from the shore just below the surface of the water that made this particular spot ideal for bluefish to congregate. The charter fishing boats that came out from the harbor routinely headed for this spot because of the concentration of fish and the assurance that their tourist customers would make their catch. Fresh bluefish, cooked over the grill, with oil and mustard sauce was a real treat for the islanders, and the bluefish were plentiful from late spring to late summer.

As Allison was daydreaming and enjoying the scenery, the boat slowed down abruptly and entered the harbor between the two stone jetties that extended out and sort of pointed back toward Hyannis. She grabbed her carry-on and went to the front of the vessel to watch the entry into the harbor. In the distance she picked out the white steeple of the Congregational Church and then, a short distance to the left, the gold dome of the Unitarian Church with the four clocks facing the four directions of the compass. The boat slowed down considerably more as it passed the sign that said "No Wake" and approached the small Brant Point Lighthouse that helped to guide boats through the harbor channel. As the boat made the turn past the lighthouse and the Coast Guard station, she could pick out the Steamship Wharf and the dock. She knew Amy and the children would be waiting on the dock, probably jumping up and down with excitement as they saw the ferry approaching. She thought to herself, *How lucky I am to have such a close friend as Amy. I never feel as if I'm a visitor, and I know she feels the same about me. Wow, do I ever need this time away!*

Dick Gimble sat down with Ed Fletcher at a small pub in Wellesley, a short distance from their office.

Ed said, "Dick, did you hear about that actuary?"

"You mean Allison Sheppard, the one who's doing the disability studies?"

"Yeah, she went off the road while riding her bike, and I heard her injuries are pretty serious."

Much of the talk around the office that morning had been about Allison's accident the night before, the fact that she had suffered a severe head injury and had been airlifted to Boston. Dick tried to act not particularly interested and replied, "I did hear the same thing and that she was still unconscious."

Dick had woken up in sort of a stupor that morning after the heavy drinking the previous evening. His sleep had been fitful, and he kept waking up asking himself, *Did I really do it, or was it a bad dream?* His emotions were torn between the violent act he had done and enormous relief over the fact that Allison's claim investigation might be dropped. He wondered initially if he had killed her, and while he felt some relief when he heard she was alive, at the same time he certainly wanted the investigation to cease. If she recovered and continued her claim study, then all of the risk he had taken the previous evening would have been for naught. However, if you could reach down into the deep recesses of his being, you would find that Dick would have been greatly relieved if she had died in the accident.

Ed said, "They say she was out riding in a park somewhere near her home and somehow lost control and went off the road into the woods. I also heard she had broken some bones."

There was a pause in their conversation, and then Ed continued, "What do you think this'll do to the investigation?"

Dick had decided not to reveal to Ed his involvement in the accident. He was sure that Ed would freak out given how nervous he had been over the claim scheme. He replied, "Hell, I don't know. I think the entire investigation was her idea and that her management didn't have it as a high priority, so maybe it'll just be forgotten. I guess it all depends on her recovery."

"Wow, what a turn of events. Maybe her misfortune will work to our benefit."

"Yeah, maybe," replied Dick. "But we probably won't know for a while when and if she can return to work. I guess if she can't go back to work, we might be able to start up our phony claim system again."

Ed thought for a minute and then said, "I don't know, Dick. I could certainly use the extra money, but I don't think I want to get back into it again. We've been damn lucky so far, and I don't know that the risk is worth the reward." He paused again, thinking, and then he continued, "I really don't want to be involved again."

Dick thought to himself, *Hell, you don't have any idea what risk is all about.* And then he replied, "Well, it's really too soon to begin to talk about resuming it anyway, but if I were sure the study had been abandoned, then I'd be ready to start again. I think our scheme is a pretty sound one, and it was really by chance that this one actuary stumbled across the problem." At this point he really didn't want to talk about it any further. His nerves were on edge, a result of the loss of sleep and the heavy drinking. He had not told Ed that he had gone back to sending in phony claims on policies that had lapsed and he had then reinstated. He knew this would spook Ed further, and he had decided that in many ways it was much easier to go it alone than involve a "nervous Eddie."

Their conversation shifted to talking about local sports, the collapse of the Red Sox in the playoffs, and the Patriots' injury to Tom Brady. Shortly after leaving the pub they went their separate ways. As they were parting, Dick said, "Let me know what else you hear about the accident."

Ed said, "Yeah, OK, I'll keep my ear to the ground. But, Dick, I really don't want to get involved in this again."

"I hear you, but we still ought to find out if she she's going to be able to return to work and resume this goddamn study."

Dick was increasingly concerned that Allison might be able to identify his car, but he knew that the whole incident had happened so quickly that it seemed unlikely. Still, he was physically shaken by what he had done the previous evening and was logically concerned about anything that might link the incident back to him. Over and over again he had gone over every detail of the "accident" to try to reassure himself that there was no way for the police to identify him. He thought to himself, *Somehow I've got to find a way to stay in touch with the actuarial department to learn if and when this investigation is resumed.*

July 2009

Jack Kendrick was not able to spend as much time on Nantucket during this summer as he had in the past and certainly less time than he truly wanted to. Both he and Amy always found the island a great relaxing getaway from the normal suburban demands and the long hours at work while at the same time raising a young family. The principal drawback of owning his own business was the fact that it required his constant attention and presence. And as a result he had much less time with Amy and the children, particularly during the summer when they spent close to three months on the island. However, he never complained since he so much enjoyed the independence and satisfaction that his photography business offered. The years he had spent as a cameraman and photographer for the TV station had been interesting and at times exciting, but his time was never his own, and if truth be known, he was often bored standing or sitting around, waiting for an event to unfold.

While the family was on the island they spoke on the phone at least once a day, and always in the evening just before the children went to bed. This time of day was truly the loneliest for Jack since he especially enjoyed playing and fooling around with the kids. It was a time to bond with them as their father, and he knew they looked forward to that time with Dad.

His workload in Boston was actually heavier during the summer since Amy was not there to relieve him at the store one day a week; in addition, the summer months were busy ones for the tourists from all over the world in the Faneuil Hall marketplace. So even though Jack ended up spending longer days at the store, the long hours helped to pass the time and push the loneliness into the background.

However, this was the July Fourth long weekend and the first long weekend Jack had spent on Nantucket since May. He was fortunate to have found a dependable part-time employee who was able to cover for him at the store in his absence.

He had arrived on Friday evening in time to enjoy a picnic at Jetties Beach and become reacquainted with the kids—he had missed them a lot since his last weekend on the island. The beach overlooked the entry to the harbor, and the boat traffic was constant, from the large steamship ferry to charter fishing boats returning with their catch to all sizes and styles of sail and motorized yachts. If the wind was right, sailboarders with as much variety in skill as in the style and color of their equipment skimmed back and forth, just out of reach of the bathers. The beach on the inside of the harbor had gentle surf, and Jeremy and Natalie loved splashing and playing in the water and the sand.

After the food was consumed and they had spent time searching the beach for some special shells or stones, they would return home somewhat exhausted and ready for bed. However, before settling down they insisted that Jack continue his usual bedtime routine of wrestling and fooling around. It seemed as though during the past year both of the children had doubled their size and certainly their agility. In the past he had to be careful in his wrestling with them not to accidently get too rough; however, now the conditions were beginning to become somewhat reversed. Both of them were physically stronger, both able to take more roughhousing and indeed give more. Amy would sometimes caution Jack not to get them too worked up for fear that they wouldn't settle down and be able to go to sleep, but on this weekend they extended their wrestling to make up for the many lost evenings over the previous several weeks.

Similar to the way Jack was always looking for and finding photo opportunities on the mainland, he always carried a camera with him wherever he went on the island. There were literally hundreds of opportunities for good shots around the island, and he knew from experience that these were big sellers at his Boston store as well as in the new shop on the island. He was always anxious to find a new picture of a scene that he had taken before, a little different angle, a different time of day with more or less shadows, and a different season of the year. Artists talked about the special light on the island for painting and photography, undoubtedly the result of being almost thirty miles in the ocean and away from smog on the mainland. Although anyone who looked at his prints would believe that he had captured almost every possible scene or setting on the island, Jack could always find something a little new and different. Each year there were subtle and sometimes major changes in the island. The winter storms and erosion frequently caused significant changes in the contour of the island, and during the past decade there had been continual erosion on the east and south coasts of the island. Several houses on the bluff in Sconset were in danger of the erosion reaching their back door and beyond. Indeed some of the homes had been moved away from the cliff in order to save them. And in Madaket, several severe storms had resulted in the erosion actually washing a few homes into the ocean. Smith's Point in Madaket was now separated from the main island, the result of a severe storm in the early 2000s.

On Saturday morning Jack took their four-wheel-drive Jeep, put the top down, and he and the kids headed out to Great Point Light on the northeast corner of the island, an area known as Coatue. Driving out to this wildlife refuge required a special permit to drive the four miles over the sand. The terrain also required lowering the air pressure in the tires to at least fifteen pounds. The Jeep was ideal for this challenge, and the two children always enjoyed the adventure, not to mention Jack himself. On this particular day he was interested in going out beyond the lighthouse to an area where there were frequently many seals. In recent years the seal population had increased, and although there were many to be found around the island in the winter months, there were also some to be found in this area of the island during the summer, lounging on the beach and basking in the sun.

Jeremy and Natalie were especially excited about seeing the seals, and of course, Jack was hopeful of getting a few good shots that he could turn into prints. The relaxed and seemingly carefree positioning of the seals made for interesting photos, and occasionally in the spring he had been successful in capturing a mother and a young pup lounging together. It was not unusual to see a dozen or more on the beach and several more close by in the water. One of Jack's best prints that was a popular seller was one where he had actually waded into the water and then caught a picture of a large seal with the lighthouse in the background.

On this particular day Jack took dozens of pictures but didn't feel that any of them were exceptional. The kids, however, enjoyed their time as well as their picnic on the beach with the wildlife. On the way back Jack spotted an osprey sitting in a nest on top of a large pole, and with his zoom lens he took several pictures in hopes there would be one he could use.

As he drove back toward town, he thought about how relaxing the few hours on the beach with his children had been. It was the first time in several weeks he had truly gotten away from his work, and he vowed to himself that he would have to find some way of getting more weekends free to come to the island.

He thought about Allison's visit with them and how fortunate she was to be recovering from her injuries with apparently no long-lasting residual effects. He was still puzzled by her accident, and even though nothing further had developed regarding her having been forced off the road, he couldn't believe that a biker as skilled as she could have had such an accident without some other factors being involved.

21

July 2009

During the months since Allison was injured, and her subsequent long recuperation and rehabilitation, Dick Gimble had frequently tried to find out if anything further was happening to the claims investigation she had started. He had lunch almost every week with his friend in the actuarial department and occasionally asked how their yearly claims studies were coming along. Anyone close to the disability business was well aware and interested in these annual studies since this analysis frequently resulted in changes in underwriting rules, premium rates, product design, and claim procedures. He also inquired about Allison's progress, and in all his inquiries he was careful not to appear too interested.

He continued to be very nervous about someone connecting him to the accident, and although he had not heard any speculation that it was anything but an unfortunate hit-and-run incident, he still experienced frequent sleepless nights. He wondered whether the police might be conducting an investigation, but there was no way for him to find out this information. As the months since the October incident passed by, he became more relaxed about the police linking him to the accident, but he still remained concerned about another actuary going further with the claim studies that Allison had begun. *Would some other actuary pick them up where Allison had left off? Just exactly what had she found out in her work? Will she be able to return to work and resume the studies, and when could that be?*

In February he had sent a get-well card to Allison and in it had written a short note: "I was so sorry to learn of your accident and especially the seriousness of your injuries, but I understand you're now making steady progress. Hope your recuperation continues at a rapid pace and look forward to seeing you back at work in the near future."

He thought that this might be still another way of keeping on top of the situation, finding out just how serious her injuries were and when she might return to work. He followed up the first card with others about every couple of weeks, and each time he included a personal note. Allison sent a reply to him after his third card, thanking him for his cards and notes and assuring him that she was indeed making good progress. She expressed her frustration at being confined and how anxious she was to return to work.

In late May, after he had sent more than a half dozen notes, he decided that if he could develop a closer relationship with Allison, then he would be better alerted to any plans she had to resume the claim study, and perhaps he'd even be able to steer her away from pursuing the study any further. He wasn't sure how he would accomplish this, but he knew that her claim study was not a high priority with actuarial management, and perhaps he could reinforce the fact that there were other studies that would be more important to the company. Perhaps he could make up some fictitious problem he was noticing in his handling of claims and suggest she should take a look at it. Claim examiners were always on the lookout for suspicious trends in claims and discussed them regularly with each other. Sometimes those concerns were geographic where, for some reason or another, there seemed to be an increase in claims from one particular part of the country. At other times, the concerns centered on a particular occupation or profession where there appeared to be a change in the normal claim activity. And sometimes their concern might be related to the frequency with which a particular type of disease or impairment was being seen in new claims.

He continued to send in phony claims on policies that had lapsed and that he had falsely reinstated, and the disability income payments continued to flow regularly into another special bank account he had set up. He had become so dependent on the increased income that there was no thought in his mind of stopping. Dick had reached the point where he had to find a way of keeping the scheme going—of keeping the money flowing in. He had not, however, considered resuming the fraudulent scheme that had attracted Allison Sheppard's attention, the scheme of sending in the phony new applications and then following them up with quick accident claims. Even though Ed Fletcher seemed to be somewhat more at ease with each passing month, he knew that he could not get him involved again even if they were convinced that there would be no further studies. As a matter of fact, Dick decided it had been a mistake to involve Ed originally. *He just doesn't have the stomach for it. I'm still worried that the dumb bastard may shoot his mouth off to someone.*

When he learned that Allison had left her parents' home and was recuperating at her apartment in Upton, he decided to inquire in one of his notes to her if she would like to go out for lunch some day if he were to drive down and pick her up. She replied to him within a week and said she'd "love to have an opportunity to get out of the apartment and get caught up on what's been going on at the company in the past several months."

Dick didn't think there was any risk in getting closer to Allison, and indeed the opportunity to know if and when she might resume the claim study overrode any fears.

During the first week of June, he drove to Upton on a Saturday and took Allison to a local pub for lunch. The drive down her street was a little eerie for him, reminding him of when he had followed her on her bike the previous October, but over lunch they both relaxed and enjoyed a light conversation. Dick learned much more about her injuries, her continuing headaches, and the gradual improvement in her leg and shoulder strength. She told him she planned to spend several weeks on Nantucket with an old college roommate and that on her return she hoped to be able to go back to work. Although she expressed interest in Dick's work and they talked about common interests in the company and mutual acquaintances, at no time did the subject of the claim investigation come up.

As Dick drove back to his apartment, he reflected on the fact that, although he hadn't learned anything new, he enjoyed his time with her and thought that she had felt the same. She was less reserved once he got to know her, and he found they had a common interest in physical fitness—hers was biking and his was a variety of sports and fitness activities. He even thought to himself, *This is really crazy, but if the circumstances were different, I could see this might develop into something serious.*

He called her the week before she left for Nantucket and arranged for another get-together, and this time he took her out for dinner at a nearby restaurant. Again there was no discussion of her actuarial work, but Dick learned more about her family and especially her friends, Amy and Jack, and their children. She was clearly excited about the vacation on Nantucket and the prospects for her continued rehabilitation in the summer sun on the island. Dick even discussed with her his separation and divorce, and said that it had been an "incompatibility issue" and that he "truly missed his children." He wondered if his comments about his children really seemed sincere because as the months had gone by since his divorce, he was seeing less and less of them. Again, as he looked back on this latest get-together with Allison, he found he had indeed enjoyed his time with her, but he was frustrated that he hadn't learned anything more about where she stood with the claim investigation.

July 2009

The summer tourist season on Nantucket was an especially busy one for the police department. The number of police personnel required to handle the summer crowds and the normal problems associated with such an inflow of tourists more than doubled the size of the department as compared to the off-season. Many of the temporary personnel were college students who had minimal training and whose jobs were primarily traffic control, parking control, patrolling, and just being visible in areas where there was a large concentration of people. Any significant or serious problems were immediately turned over to an experienced and trained officer or detective.

However, this put a real strain on the trained year-round staff who had to be available to handle the normal increase in crime that came with such an increase in population. Many of the problems involved young people charged with disorderly conduct, usually associated with excessive use of alcohol. There was also the expected increase in the number of auto accidents and instances of driving while under the influence that one would expect with a population five times greater than normal. Some of the worst accidents, however, involved mopeds rented by tourists who had little familiarity with the vehicles and consequently found themselves in situations where they lost control and ended up with broken arms, legs, or if they were lucky, only a roadburn from falling and skidding along the asphalt.

Al Collins truly hated this time of year because of the increased pressure of his job and the number of overtime hours he was expected to put in. There just never seemed to be enough hours in the day to stay ahead of the multitude of problems that occurred. During nine months of the year he felt pretty much in control of the issues that he had to deal with as the senior detective, but during the summer he was simply overwhelmed. He was the type of person who functioned best when he was dealing with a small number of problems, ones that he could see his way to resolving in a short period of time. This summer was a particularly frustrating one since, along with the expected increase in police activity, he still had to deal with the growing and unsolved problem of break-ins that had occurred during the winter months.

The chief had insisted a couple of months previously that he bring in the state police to help in the investigation, and this had been a blow to Al's ego. But the truth was that there had been little progress in the investigation, and the public was getting increasingly impatient. The number of break-ins continued during the summer; however, they were discovered more quickly because the seasonal homes, vacant in the winter, were now occupied. The other thing that had changed was that where the thefts during the winter were primarily the more expensive electronic items such as TVs and stereo components, most of the thefts during the summer were jewelry and other smaller items of value that the seasonal residents had brought to the island for their vacations. Laptop computers and small electronic gadgets such as iPods and BlackBerries left in the house while the residents went off to the beach, out to dinner, or to some other event on the island were increasingly items of choice for the thieves. Vacationers on a peaceful isle frequently neglected to lock their doors or turn on their security systems, part of the natural relaxation of a summer holiday. There had been a few arrests, many of them young people, but the number of cases continued to increase over previous years, and the state police were convinced they were dealing with some sophisticated criminals, not just the young, inexperienced element. The state police had mentioned to Al that the pattern seemed to follow those seen in other areas of the state, where the thefts were linked to individuals who were trying to raise money to pay for their drug habits.

They questioned him about secondhand stores on the island and if he had checked them out to see if any of the stolen goods were there. He was pissed off that they would question him on something so basic to good police investigation and had replied, "Look, first of all this is a small island and there is only one secondhand store. Second, anyone would be a fool to try to sell stolen goods on an island this small. They'd be certain to be found out. And finally, yes, I checked out that store, and although they do carry some TVs, stereos, and other electronic stuff, there's no evidence whatsoever of any of the goods being there."

Al knew Tony Andrews well. They had been in school together and played in the same softball league. Al said, "I know the owner well, and he wouldn't be stupid enough to try to sell stolen property."

It was clear that the stolen goods had to be shipped off the island since there was too great a risk of being caught if they tried to unload them on the island, and Al had been encouraged to look into how these goods, especially the large items, were taken off the island. Obviously it had to be in vehicles that left on the steamship ferry, but what kind of vehicle would likely carry the goods—large trucks, pickup trucks, vans? With the help of the state police they had concluded that it was probably a closed and somewhat inconspicuous panel truck of some kind, and one that made trips off island on a regular basis.

On this particular day Al had been looking over several lists of trucks that had gone on the ferry since the beginning of the year. He was frustrated that nothing really jumped out at him as a likely possibility. However, he had made a list of more than fifty vehicles that regularly traveled on the ferry back and forth to Hyannis. He wasn't sure where to go next. He'd like to be able to check all of the trucks before they were loaded, but this involved getting court permission and would greatly interfere with the steamship schedule. Somehow he had to narrow down the list to a more manageable number. His reduced staff, truly no staff at all during the summer months, resulted in the problem being squarely in his lap. Detective Dick Hines, whom he depended on for help during the fall, winter, and spring months, was too busy doing regular police work during the summer and could not help him with the investigation.

As he sat at his desk pondering what his next move would be, his phone rang. He was told that there had been a serious accident involving multiple cars and injuries on Old South Road, but all of the other police officers were tied up with other duties. As he left his office, he said to himself, *Oh shit, how am I supposed to solve this goddamn case if I'm continually pulled away? Why doesn't the town recognize that we're really understaffed?* However, if the truth were known, Al was secretly glad to get away from the break-in problem since he didn't have any idea what steps to take next in the investigation.

July 2009

Tony Andrews's secondhand business was especially busy during the summer months. As the seasonal residents came to the island to open up their homes and cottages, they frequently brought with them new furniture they had purchased off island and discarded the old. From the middle of April through the early part of July, there was a steady stream of people wanting to unload a various assortment of used furniture and household items. At the same time, the year-round residents, being aware of the annual ritual, would show up in large numbers to try to find a bargain on some secondhand item that had been gently used and would cost many times as much if they were to purchase it new.

Tony knew he was offering a valuable service to both ends of the transaction, and it was during this time of year when he made most of his secondhand business profits.

However, his real income increasingly came from the drug trade. Like most items for sale on this expensive island, in the summer the demand for drugs increased with the population growth, and consequently the prices went up. He had to be careful to have enough supply for his regular customers and, in fact, gave them a little break on the prices, but he had to be especially careful about dealing with any new drug customers who were unknown to him. There were some users who showed up every summer, customers he knew and felt safe with; however, he refused to deal with anyone new unless they were brought to him by someone he knew and could trust. As his drug business grew, he naturally became more and more concerned about his risks. *Will one of these customers be caught in a break-in and turn me in? Will one of the users be caught with drugs and under police pressure give out my name? Is it possible that one of my new customers, even though I try to be careful as hell, might be an undercover cop and set me up?*

However, with each passing month and year he had not only become somewhat more blasé about the risk, but if the truth be known, he subconsciously enjoyed the high of the risk—something like the high that many people get when they participate in extreme sports. In addition, he naturally became more and more dependent on the income from his drug business, very substantial income indeed that dwarfed the income from the secondhand business. Up until this point, the only scare he had received was a visit by the local police in early May when they explained to him that the state police believed that the items stolen over the winter might show up in his secondhand store for sale. They were quick to add that they weren't accusing or suspecting him of knowingly receiving stolen property, but that he might unknowingly be the victim of having bought a used TV or stereo from someone that he thought was legitimate.

They had come in with a long, three-page list of items, TVs, stereo systems, DVD players, and other electronic gadgets that had been stolen over the winter, some with detailed descriptions that included size, style, make, and any unique features. He looked over the list and commented to the police that many of the items and descriptions were pretty standard ones, but he emphasized that he just didn't carry many secondhand electronic products. He had, in fact, recognized many of the items on the police list as ones he had received and sold off island, but at no time did the police even suggest or question him about any items he may have taken off island. It was apparent they had assumed his frequent trips off island were solely to purchase items that he would turn around and sell back on Nantucket.

Of course, the fact that the detective, Al Collins, was someone he had known for years made Tony feel especially invulnerable. Al sort of approached the whole situation somewhat casually, apologizing for even having to bother Tony, and had said, "Look, Tony, the state police are now involved in this break-in investigation and are making me go through some hoops that I know are a waste of time, but I have so many people breathing down my neck I don't have a choice. So just bear with me while I go through the routine."

Tony quickly said, "Yeah, Al, I know you've been under a lot of pressure, and I'll help out in any way I can, but I want you to know I'm really careful about who I do business with, and I don't believe I have any of the items you're talking about." And then he added, trying to cover himself if by chance someone should give his name in the future, "I suppose it's possible that somewhere along the line I might receive some of this stolen stuff, but it would be the exception, not the rule. You know, Al, with the large number of items on this list, there's no way they're all still on the island."

Al replied, "We know that most of the items couldn't be sold here, but we haven't yet been able to identify who's taking them off island. They're obviously going by some kind of truck on the ferry, but with hundreds of vehicles going every week, it's like looking for a needle in a haystack."

Then Al thought to himself, *Maybe Tony can be some help here.* "Tony, if someone was trying to unload some hot items off island, where would they go?"

Tony was startled by Al's question, but he composed himself and hesitated before answering. "Wow, you're asking me something that I've never thought about. It's an area that I just wouldn't know where to begin. The people I deal with are legitimate antique or second-hand dealers, and I'm positive they aren't involved in illegal stuff."

He thought further, *Maybe I can steer him away from my off-island sources in New Bedford and Brockton.* And he added, "I suppose that the big cities, like Boston and Providence, must have some of these shady dealers. As a matter of fact, you know all the jokes about the Mafia in Rhode Island, so I might look there first." Tony chuckled and felt a little proud of himself that he had mentioned the most logical cities that might be the source, but he had avoided the ones where his illegal dealers were actually located. Still, he felt uncomfortable about Al Collins's questions.

Al said, "Yeah, I guess it's logical that a large city is where you'd expect most of the illegal activity to take place. Well, thanks for your time, Tony. Sorry to bother you, but if anything comes to mind where you think you can help me or if you hear anything, give me a call."

"Of course I will, Al."

As Al Collins left, Tony stood and looked after the cruiser as it turned down the road toward town. He was by nature sort of a cocky individual and said to himself, *I think I pulled that off really well. There's no way he can possibly be suspicious of what's going on here. I'm lucky that I'm dealing with Al and not some state cop. Nevertheless, I'd better be extra careful about who I do business with.*

24

July 2009

As had become her normal routine, Amy Kendrick arrived at her photo shop on the pier at nine o'clock in the morning, and for the first hour she was kept busy looking over the sales results from the previous day. She and her business partner, Kathy Abraham, had opened up the shop on Memorial Day weekend and then for three days each weekend during the month of June as the summer visitors began to pick up in numbers. However, from the first week of July they were open from nine in morning to nine at night, seven days a week, and that schedule was to continue until Labor Day. Sales of both photos and paintings had begun very slowly, but with the advent of July Fourth things had truly begun to pick up. It was too early to tell whether the venture was going to be a success, but as they approached the middle of July, they both were encouraged. Some days there was little activity, but then other days, especially weekends, would more than make up for it. Like most shops in tourist communities, rainy weather meant a poor beach day and resulted in more activity in the shops.

The schedule for Amy was a demanding one, but so far it had been manageable. She was there five days each week from nine until one o'clock, then Kathy took over until five o'clock, and finally the local teacher they had hired, Patti Gross, took the final four hours until nine o'clock. On the weekends they shifted the schedule so that Patti worked two shifts each day and Amy and Kathy each had a day off.

It required a lot of juggling for Amy around caring for the children. Her normal weekday routine was to get the children to an island summer camp program before she went to the shop, and then they spent the afternoon and evening doing the typical things that vacationing families on the island did. The summer camp program was one that both Jeremy and Natalie looked forward to, and it was one that combined arts and crafts activities along with some local history. They visited the local windmill and saw how wheat was ground into flour, and then they even took some of the flour and made muffins. They visited one of the lighthouses and learned how it operated and why they were so important to sailors before navigational electronics and GPS systems became commonplace on even smaller vessels. They were told how the ancient whalers would work with whale teeth and bone and design all kinds of items of scrimshaw, and then the children were given a piece of imitation bone material to make their own scrimshaw. Each day Jeremy and Natalie would come home with some article that they had made, proud to show it to their mother.

In the afternoon, assuming that the weather cooperated, Amy and the kids would head off to one of the many beaches. When the children were younger, their favorite spot was Children's Beach, which was in the inner harbor, a beach with hardly any surf that also had a play yard with all sorts of jungle gym equipment, slides, and swings. However, during the last couple of years they had begun to outgrow that beach and now favored either Jetties or Dionis Beach. Both were on the north side of the island, away from the high surf of the south coast, and they had the advantage of gently sloping beaches for the children to play in or out of the water.

Now that the children were ages four and six, Amy found she had more time to herself at the beach. Rather than having to play with the children constantly, she found they could amuse themselves on their own, either in the water or playing in the sand. During the last two weeks since Allison had arrived, she found this time sitting on the beach was especially enjoyable as they visited, reminisced, laughed at the children's antics, and simply relished in each other's company.

She was pleased to see how far Allison had come in her recovery and how positive she was about being able to return to work in a few weeks. They talked about Amy's business venture, how Jack's store in Boston was doing, and Allison even mentioned the increased contact she had had with Dick Gimble. Amy kidded her about the relationship and tried to probe and learn if Allison truly had an interest in him. Allison was reluctant to talk much about Dick, but the fact that she had brought him into the conversation meant to Amy that this might grow into something more serious.

On other afternoons, when the weather wasn't conducive to sitting on the beach, there were always a variety of other activities available. One of the things the children truly enjoyed was driving out to one of the small ponds in Madaket and "fishing" for turtles. It was a pond where there was an abundance of fairly large snapping turtles, and if you tied a string to a chicken leg and dangled it in the water, you were usually rewarded with a sharp pull as a turtle grabbed hold, tugging, and sometimes even holding on while you tried to pull it up onto the dock. If you were successful, the turtle would quickly let go of the chicken and scoot back into the water. In the course of an hour or so, each child could go through several pieces of chicken until the turtles became full, the children ran out of chicken legs, or both became tired of the game.

Although the commitment to the shop made this summer's schedule an especially busy one, Amy enjoyed the challenge of the new venture, getting back into the working world and having time away from the role of mother for at least some part of the day. In addition to Jack's evening call to the children, he and Amy would talk on the phone each day while she was at the shop as to what was selling and what they could do to increase sales. After a few weeks Amy began to get a better feel for which items the public truly liked, and she rearranged things in the store to showcase those photographs. Some items actually sold out very quickly, and it was somewhat of a struggle to keep those popular ones in supply. When Jack made a weekend trip to the island, he routinely packed his car full of those items that were in demand.

Kathy Abraham's artwork did not generate the number of sales as Amy's photos; however, Kathy's paintings were much more expensive, so a few sales each week generated enough income to satisfy her needs. Her total income through the middle of July was significantly less than what Amy's was; however, she was selling more than she had in previous years. They had agreed to split the rental expense of the shop according to the sales, so Amy was paying approximately two-thirds of the rent and Kathy the rest. One of the important and somewhat sensitive areas they had to deal with was the amount of space each used to display artwork and how they allocated the more favorable display areas. Fortunately, they recognized each other's needs and found ways of resolving these thorny issues before they grew into problems.

As Amy was rearranging displays in the store this particular morning, she thought about how quickly the summer weeks were passing, and she resolved to make certain she took the time to enjoy the many activities the island offered.

July 2009

Allison had been on the island for two weeks and increasingly felt this had been the right decision to finalize her recovery before returning to work. She not only enjoyed the time she spent with Amy and Jack's children and the evenings when she and Amy simply sat around and talked, but she also found the time to get away by herself and begin to rejuvenate her enthusiasm and excitement about the future. Those days and weeks following the accident when she feared she would be unable to resume her normal life were now fears that were fading into the background.

Her headaches had diminished in number and intensity, and she had continued to gain back the strength in her arms and legs. She had fallen into a routine of riding a bike one morning and then jogging the next. She had gradually increased the length of the bike rides to more than five miles, and on one occasion she had gone to the end of the island in Sconset, a round trip of almost fifteen miles. She had not resumed the speed at which she used to ride but rather kept to a gradual pace, giving herself time to build up her muscles and her confidence. The many bike paths on the island made bike riding a lot safer than having to negotiate narrow roads with heavy summer traffic. The scenery and quietness on the rides, especially early in the morning, were stimulating. And although she had never really enjoyed swimming, she looked forward to the invigorating daily dips in the cool summer ocean in the afternoon or evening.

She found herself thinking more and more about returning to work and what lay ahead of her. She thought about her next actuarial exams and when she could begin her study schedule, and thankfully she found the problem of being unable to concentrate for long periods of time began to improve.. She frequently thought about her claim analysis studies and especially the gnawing problem of the increase in accident claims. Even though it was not a major financial concern for the company at this point, her nature was such that she hated to be faced with a problem that she couldn't resolve. She also knew that if the trend of these accident claims continued, then at some point it would become a serious enough problem for senior management to be concerned.

She had brought her laptop computer with her and previously had downloaded the files that she needed to do some further evaluation. So during the second week of her stay on Nantucket, she found a few hours where she got back into the claim evaluation materials and refreshed her memory about what she had discovered previously. The fact that the problem was centered in the northeast part of the country and that the claims occurred on recently approved policies was of particular concern. Whenever a claim occurred shortly after the policy had been approved, insurance companies became suspicious that the policyholder might have applied for the insurance with the plan to submit a quick claim. Most often these types of quick claims were for some sickness that the individual knew he or she had and was likely to have need for the insurance. If the company had been told about the condition, they frequently would not provide coverage for that specific disease, but in this instance the claims were for accidents, things that an individual could not anticipate in advance. The nature of legitimate accident claims was that they were just that, unanticipated events that one could not predict. The only way one could plan for submitting an accident claim would be to fake an injury and submit a phony claim. But how could so many people in one small geographic area be submitting fraudulent accident claims? Allison was puzzled. She wasn't sure of what her next step would be, but she knew it had to involve digging deeper behind these policies and claims to determine if there were other similarities that might lead to some logical explanation.

Occasionally during the past few weeks she had thought about Dick Gimble and the contact she had had with him since the accident. She had enjoyed his attention, and he seemed genuinely interested in her and her accident, but she was somewhat apprehensive because she knew he had recently been through a divorce, and by nature she was a person who moved ahead in her personal relationships very cautiously. Her life for the past several years had first involved college and studying, and then since graduation the demands of her job, especially studying for her actuarial exams, and consequently left little time for her social life. She had always been shy in her contacts with the opposite sex and had never truly had a serious relationship. The only "boyfriend" she had had was in high school when she and a classmate who shared the same interests, and whom she referred to as "another math geek," would team up together when there was a school dance or some other occasion for couples. It never blossomed into a romance, and they had gone their separate ways after high school.

In college Amy had tried on a few occasions to fix Allison up so that they could double date, but Allison's shyness and serious focus on her studies never allowed these contacts to develop into anything further. Now in her early thirties there were times when she thought about her future, something beyond her actuarial profession. She looked at Amy and Jack and their children and had some envy of their relationship and their lifestyle. At times she thought it would be nice to have a more complete life, at least by today's American standards, and she knew that her biological clock was ticking as far as having children. But since she had set her mind during college on her professional goal of becoming a fellow of the Society of Actuaries, she had put other interests aside as things that would have to wait. There was still time to consider marriage and a family, and there were times when she would honestly say to herself, *Perhaps marriage isn't for me. I'm happy and challenged in my profession, and I'm not going to be pushed into some relationship just because society says it's the right thing to do.*

So although she was intrigued with the attention she had received from Dick Gimble, it was not something that she was terribly excited about or anything that she dreamed about developing into a serious relationship. Her job and her career were the things that continued to dominate her thoughts and her plans for the future.

July 2009

Jack's weekend had been one of the most relaxing ones he had
had in several months. It was so important for him to spend
good chunks of time with the kids, and he found that his involvement with their activities was perhaps the best way to entirely take
his mind off the responsibilities of his store back in Boston. The
July Fourth celebrations in the downtown area of Nantucket, along
with the fireworks that evening, were such exciting events for the
kids that Jack found himself so wrapped up in their enthusiasm
that it didn't matter he had probably seen both events at least a
dozen times previously.

On Sunday evening Jack and Amy had gone out to the Sea
Grill for dinner, and Allison had stayed at home with Jeremy and

Natalie. He and Amy had an opportunity to catch up on some of the details that one missed when trying to communicate over the telephone. They talked about the children's activities during the summer, about Jeremy starting the first grade in the fall, and Natalie continuing in day care a few days a week. Like most parents, they showed interest and some anxiety about how their first child would make out in the full day of public school. They thought that Jeremy had progressed well in kindergarten, but they knew that much more was expected of children much sooner than when they had gone to school. They talked about his first-grade teacher, someone they didn't know personally but had heard fairly good reports about from some of their friends. It was important and good therapy for them to listen to each other's thoughts and thereby reassure each other that they were on the same page.

They discussed both the store in Boston and the new venture on Nantucket. Amy's excitement over how the sales were going, even though it was early in the season, was obvious in her voice. Jack was especially pleased that this was going well, not so much from a financial point of view, but rather that Amy's enthusiasm relieved his concern that the store might have been too much for her and might have ruined the traditional summer on the island that she had been used to. He brought her up to date on what was happening at the Boston store, the items that were selling best, some of the interesting customers he had come in contact with, and of course, how the business as a whole was doing financially. They had both been concerned about how he would be able to handle all of the additional tasks that Amy usually took responsibility for when she was back in Boston. Although their lives were very full and busy with the business and with the normal cares and concerns of most young families, they both realized how very fortunate they were in their marriage, their family, and their business.

This kind of evening, away from the day-to-day responsibilities of family and business, was a very special occasion for both of them. They truly enjoyed each other's company, and they discussed many other things over dinner and a glass or two of wine.

Amy said, "I really think Allison is making great progress. She's been jogging and biking and says that her headaches have almost entirely disappeared."

"Well, that's good to hear. What does she say about going back to work?"

"Well, she's been doing some work while she's been here—I guess mostly on some claim study that she's really interested in. Her doctor told her that she can probably go back full time in September. I've been trying to convince her to stay here a couple of weeks longer, perhaps to the middle of August."

"I'm glad the two of you have had this time together, and she certainly seems to be enjoying herself."

"Yeah, well, you know we're truly like sisters. She's really been a great help, especially in looking after the kids when I've been busy. So I do hope she'll stay a while longer."

"I'm glad it's going along well, but I wish I could be down here more. I miss you and the kids, even though I'm busy at work."

"You know that I miss you too, and the kids would love to have you around. I kind of look at this summer as a unique one and not how it's going to be in the future. When the business gets more established, I think you'll feel you can leave it for longer periods of time."

"Yeah, I know, and the fall will be here soon, and then we'll all be back together."

"We'll make up for lost time."

Later that evening, back at the cottage, Jack got into a discussion with Allison about her accident. Up until that time all of the information he had heard about the accident and her injuries had come from Amy. Being a person addicted to reading mystery novels, he was naturally interested in learning more about the details first-hand. Even though Allison was initially somewhat reticent about discussing all of her thoughts and concerns, Jack was not bashful about probing and asking questions.

After Jack had finally, through persistent questioning, obtained many more details than he had known previously, he commented, "You know, Allison, you're a really experienced biker, and I don't think there's any way you could have gone off the road without something else being involved. And I just can't imagine someone causing an accident and not stopping to see if they could help. Even if they're worried about being at fault, the basic human instinct would be to see what they could do to help, to see if you'd been injured. It's a pretty coldhearted person who does a hit-and-run."

"Yeah, I know what you mean. I've thought a lot about what kind of a person would just leave me on the side of the road. I could have died."

"You said you thought it was a car and perhaps a green one?"

"Uh huh, that's about the most I can remember, and that's not very clear in my mind. It all happened so fast. You know that the police took my bike and checked for any signs of green paint and it came up negative?"

Jack replied, "Amy had mentioned that to me. I know that the details of the accident gradually came back to you over several weeks after your injuries, but have you remembered anything further recently?"

"No, it's been several months now since I've remembered anything more. I think that's it. You know it all happened so quickly, and I'm sure I was so busy trying to control the bike that I wouldn't have had time to look back at the car."

"Well, it sure was a hell of an experience, and thankfully you're making a great recovery."

"Well, the time I'm spending here has really been good for me. I can't thank you and Amy enough. I've relaxed and gotten some good exercise, and I've found that I can go for a full day and not even think about the accident. I'm really feeling great."

"Amy says she's suggested that you stay on into August, and I hope you will. She's really enjoying your company."

"It's nice of both of you to offer, and I'll probably take you up on it."

Dick Gimble and Ed Fletcher had just finished playing a softball game in an area league that included some ten different companies. Dick was the better player of the two, but both of them enjoyed the physical activity and the friendly, competitive atmosphere. Dick had driven in the winning run in the last inning and was still sky high over the victory.

"Wow! I was lucky to get that final hit. Their pitcher had pretty much shut us down, and I had done nothing until that last at bat."

"Yeah, I didn't even get a foul ball off that guy. You really clobbered that last pitch. It wasn't luck at all."

Dick replied, "Well, he really had my number for the rest of the night, but it sure did feel good to get at least one off of him."

"Did you see the look on those guys' faces after that hit? You know they're a real cocky group."

"Well that pays them back a little for the clobbering they gave us the last time we played them."

After they put their gear into the trunk and settled into Dick's car, Ed said, "What have you heard about the actuary who was hurt and the claim study?"

Dick replied, "Funny you should ask. I've been keeping in touch with her pretty regularly, and she seems to be coming along quite well."

"What do you mean, 'keeping in touch with her'?"

"Well, I'd sent her a couple of cards while she was recovering, and back a few weeks ago I gave her a call. And after that I actually took her out to lunch."

"You're kidding me."

"No, and in fact, a couple of weeks later I took her out a second time. I thought it was a good way to stay on top of what's happening with the claim study, especially since I wasn't able to learn anything from anyone else."

"You've got a hell of a lot of nerve, Dick. Well, what have you learned?"

"Right now she's on Nantucket vacationing with a friend of hers, and I guess she'll be there for a few weeks. As near as I can tell, nothing further has happened with the claim study, but I've been very careful not to ask too many questions. She's still recovering from the accident and doesn't plan to go back to work until the fall."

"Do you think she'll pick up the study again then?"

Dick said, "I don't really know, and she hasn't said anything about it, but as I told you before, this doesn't seem to be a big priority in the minds of actuarial management. I think she'll be busy with other things and this'll just die."

"Even though we haven't sent in any more apps or claims since the end of last year, I'm still nervous about it. It's been a real stretch for me without the extra money we were getting, but I'm glad we stopped when we did."

Of course, Ed was still not aware that Dick was still sending in phony claims, and in fact Dick was actually bringing in more money for himself than before.

Dick said, "I plan to continue to stay close to Allison, and I'll let you know if anything develops."

In a sort of teasing voice, Ed said, "Sounds to me as though this may be something more, Dick. What's she like anyway?"

Dick hesitated and then said, "Well, she's really a nice person. Quiet and a bit shy, but once you get to know her, she opens up a little more. If the situation was different, I might really get interested in her."

"Hey, maybe you can get her into bed and take her mind off the study permanently."

Dick, still serious, said, "I don't think that's in the cards, but who knows what may happen down the road. The closer I get the more I can learn about her work."

In spite of his comments to Ed, Dick was uneasy about Allison's return to work and whether she would pick up on the study where she'd left off. He also knew that he was running additional risks as he continued to send in false claims on those policies that he had reinstated. So far he had been lucky, and he continued to be careful to submit claims that he believed had a low chance of being investigated. That was the key! He had to be careful not to get too greedy. Many of the phony claims he had handled himself, but it was the other ones that worried him. He kept track of every one when the paperwork arrived in the office, and even on those that were handled by another examiner, Dick would regularly check to see that the claim was being processed without any hitches.

With each passing week and month he dug a deeper hole for himself, becoming ever more dependent on the extra money. With Ed out of the picture and with the fear that his new scheme would be discovered, Dick had scaled back the number of phony claims but was still bringing in more than five thousand dollars each month, sixty thousand dollars a year tax free. He had paid all of his past bills, had nothing due on his credit cards, and had even put away several thousand dollars in a savings account. At times he thought about backing off the scheme a little, but then the thrill of the risk gave him such a high that he quickly put any thought of stopping behind him.

28

July 2009

Dick Gimble gave Tony Andrews a call on the phone. Although they'd had little contact with each other for more than a decade, they had become quite close in college. While Tony had flunked out of the college in his second year, Dick after two years had transferred to the larger four-year state university and received his degree.

They had roomed together for the first two years, and Dick was well aware of Tony's lucrative side business dealing in drugs. Dick himself had played around with drugs, but never enough to get hooked. He had always been quite rigidly disciplined when it came to being in control of his own physical shape. Marijuana, as was the case in other schools, was easy to come by at the small college and could frequently be found at weekend parties; Tony was often the supplier.

One long spring weekend during those two years, Dick had gone to Nantucket with Tony and had been given the special native's tour of the island, one that hit the spots that only a person who grew up on the island would think to show someone. Tony showed him some of the out-of-the-way places where he and his buddies had partied during high school, away from adult interference. Looking back on that weekend, Dick was sure they must have driven dozens of miles on unpaved roads, many where you needed a four-wheel-drive vehicle or else you ran the risk of getting stuck in the sand. Even though it was too early to take a swim, Tony had taken him to some of the more secluded beaches that the year-round residents frequented that were not crowded in the summer with tourists. And along the way Tony relayed stories of various incidents he and his friends had experienced as teenagers, most of them hell-raising and some of them clearly outside of the law. He took great pleasure in poking fun at the police department and bragged about how much they had gotten away with, and as Dick suspected, many of the incidents involved exploits with drugs and girls.

One of the places Dick still vividly remembered was the drive out on the sand to the Great Point Lighthouse, and then they continued on over the sand on an arm of the island called Coatue that curved back some six miles to a point that overlooked the harbor toward the town center. They must have traveled at least fifteen miles over the sand until they finally got back to the paved road at Wauwinet. Along the way they ran across dozens of angry seagulls who were trying to protect their newly born chicks from the intrusion. A couple of times they got out of their Jeep and tried to get near the nests, but the noise and aggressive behavior of the seagulls kept them from getting close.

His visit had been during the last weekend in April, which was also the annual Daffodil Festival weekend celebration, and Dick had been treated to the events of the first tourist weekend of the season. On Saturday morning Main Street was closed from the lower end up to the Pacific Bank building, and by eleven o'clock the street was clogged with close to a hundred antique autos of all shapes and sizes, some from the 1920s vintage. Many were decorated with daffodils, and the dress of the day included just about anything as long as it was yellow. Perhaps the most startling items of dress were the vast array of hats. Some of them were wildly decorated with artificial daffodils, many on the garish side, but all were done in the spirit of the day. Strollers with children, young people on bikes, and dogs of every variety were decked out in yellow. Some of the antique vehicles had been modified or souped up, but all seemed to be in relatively good condition.

At noontime the parade of autos was led by an antique fire engine through town and then out Milestone Road for the seven miles to Sconset. Hundreds of thousands of daffodils lined the road to Sconset along with the spectators. Many tourists and locals had preceded the parade out to the small village on the most eastern point of the island, staking out a piece of lawn to watch the parade as it arrived. Dick was amazed at the elaborate lunches, gourmet buffets in some instances, which people had set up along the side of the road. It was truly a festive occasion, the signal on the island of the arrival of spring and the anticipation of the summer tourist season to come.

After passing the time of day over the phone and catching up on what was generally going on in each of their lives, Dick said, "Tony, I was wondering, could I stay with you for a couple of days if I came down to the island?"

Tony hesitated for a minute. Anyone who had a home on the island was never without visitors during the summer, and sometimes the large number of them really got out of control. In Tony's case, he had the added complication of his business being run from his residence, and he was always sensitive to anyone getting too close to his operation. Dick, however, had been a close friend and knew about his illegal drug activities from college. He replied, "Sure, I'd like to get together and relive some old times, Dick. When were you thinking you'd come?"

"Well, I'm not exactly sure yet. There's a girl I work with who's vacationing there, and I thought I'd surprise her and come down for a couple of days, but I've got to check and make sure she'll be there."

"So you're not coming down to spend some time with an old friend, but because you've got the hots for some chick."

Dick chuckled a bit. "Yeah, I guess that's right, but believe it or not, I'd really like to catch up on what you've been up to. It's been several years since we've seen each other."

Tony, still teasing Dick, said, "Oh sure, don't give me that bullshit. Is this something serious? I thought you were married."

"Well, I was, but I got divorced a few years ago. Just didn't work out. But this girl I'm talking about was in a serious accident last year and is still recuperating. We've had a couple of dates, but nothing serious."

"Sure. But it's a long way to come for nothing serious. Well, maybe something will blossom when you're here."

"Yeah, well look, Tony, is there any time in the next couple of weeks that's not good for you?"

"No, during the summer my business is such that I'm here all the time. Give me a call when you know."

"Thanks, Tony, and I'll only be there for a couple of days."

Tony laughed and said, "I've heard that one before."

29

July 2009

For a few hours during the past several days, Allison had once again begun to delve into the claim study. Having been away from it for almost a year, it took her some time to familiarize herself with all of the detail and the questions she had raised previously. She took several hours going over all the data she had accumulated and revisiting the assumptions and initial concerns she had developed. In addition, she now had all of the claim results from the year 2008 to bring into the study that were not available when she last looked at the data.

She had brought down to Nantucket the computer disc with all the previous information on the claim study, made some calls back to the company, and was able to access the new data she needed and download it onto her laptop computer. The more data she had to work with, the more reliable the conclusions she could reach. She wondered whether the 2008 data would show the same trend with the accident claims, or whether a lack of evidence of the same trend would prove that it had been a statistical aberration.

Once all of the new data had been combined with her original data, Allison began to go back to determine whether the same trends did, in fact, exist. It became quickly evident that the numbers of accident claims for the year 2008 were also running considerably higher than had been expected. As a matter of fact, the variance from what was projected by the actuarial assumptions was almost identical to the previous four years of her study. This, in itself, was unusual since there normally is some degree of variation from year to year. The concern was not that there was a variance, but rather the degree of variance and the trends, and here again in each of the five years the number of accident claims in the northeastern part of the country, especially in New England, considerably exceeded what was expected. She was even more convinced that it just didn't make sense. *Something strange is going on here that can't be explained by normal statistical variance, and it's continuing.*

She confirmed again that the claims were all of relatively short durations, only four or five weeks of disability, and the monthly indemnity payments were relatively small, from one thousand to two thousand dollars per month. The claims were all on recently approved policies, and the claims were usually submitted in the first two or three months after the policies had been issued. And finally, all of the policies lapsed within a month after the last claim payment was made. Allison said to herself, *There're just too many coincidences. The patterns over the five-year period are just too definite. Never mind that the claims are way out of proportion to the rest of the country, claims just don't behave that consistently.*

Even though the typical total claim payment for each of the claims she identified was not huge, when you totaled up the effect of all of these claims on an annual basis, the amount totaled more than a hundred thousand dollars each year. This was a small fraction of the more than one hundred and fifty million dollars annually paid out in disability claims by John Adams Insurance, but it was still something that Allison knew needed to be understood. And she noticed other patterns that were just too consistent. The applications had all been made through the new electronic application system where everything was done over the Internet, and it appeared that a new application for a different person was submitted about every week throughout the year. When she looked at the nature of the disability that resulted in the claim, here again there were similarities—knee and back injuries being the most common, frequently the result of a supposed auto accident. As she looked at other data, she found that the claimants were almost all in their thirties or forties.

Allison became more and more convinced that there must be some kind of fraud scheme involved. *There's simply no way this number of coincidences could randomly occur. Someone's been working some kind of scheme to steal from the company, and even though it's not millions of dollars, maybe it's just the tip of the iceberg.*

She began to think about how such a scheme could be pulled off without the perpetrator being caught. All of the claims required some medical proof of disability, and many claims were even investigated, but she was pretty certain that the fact that these particular disabilities were fairly short in duration with relatively small claim payments probably meant minimal investigation. *I'll need to pull out the actual claim files and see if there are any other similar patterns. If one person is behind this, and these are all phony applicants, how come the underwriting investigation didn't smell out a problem? Here again, maybe the small size of the application didn't necessitate further underwriting investigation. I wonder if the underwriting procedures on electronic applications are different. I need to ask some questions and find out some of the underwriting rules and guidelines. And how about the claim department? How could all of these claims get through without some investigation? Did they check with any of the physicians listed on the claim forms, or don't they investigate the smaller claims?*

She made a telephone call to Bill Alberti, her manager in the actuarial department, and told him what more she had found and what she suspected. She asked him if he could have someone pull out some of the actual claim files for her to examine further. He was so consumed with much larger problems, many involving tens of millions of dollars, that he hesitated before agreeing to let Allison dig deeper into her study. He knew she was tenacious, and he did not want to appear uncooperative, especially given her own long disability and recovery and the fact that he had agreed to let her pursue the study during her rehabilitation.

"Look, Allison, that certainly sounds like something suspicious, but we've talked before about the fact that the total loss to the company is still fairly small in the large scheme of things. You know we've got other studies going on with much more at stake for the company, and I don't want to use important resources in chasing down claims or applications that I could be putting to better use elsewhere."

Allison replied, "I understand, Bill, but I really think this is a case of fraud, and it may get even bigger if we don't figure out what's going on. It's sure not just a statistical aberration, and even though it may not be as large a problem as others, it's getting close to a half-million-dollar loss for the company over the five-year period I've been looking at."

Bill replied, "Well look, Allison, I know this is important to you, and I'm really pleased to see you back at work and being able to concentrate on things without the headache problems you've been having. I'm hesitant to ask the claim or underwriting departments to free up their resources to look at claims and applications, but I suppose I could pull say a couple of dozen of each without upsetting anyone."

"Well, that's certainly a start, and hopefully I'll be able to find something that begins to unravel this mystery. I really appreciate it."

"Why don't you send me a list of the claims and applications you want to look at, and I'll have someone pull them and then either e-mail or mail them to you."

"That would be great, Bill. I'll look over what I've got and get you the list in the next few days."

"OK, but remember it may take a little while to get back to you."

"Fine."

"I'm really glad to see you're doing so much better, Allison, and we're all looking forward to your getting back here full time. There are some important projects that I'd really like to get you involved in."

"Yeah, I can't tell you how anxious I am to get back."

July 2009

It was getting toward the end of July and had been almost three weeks since Jack had been on Nantucket for the Fourth of July. He was looking forward to getting back to the island this coming weekend and spending time with Amy and the kids. The daily phone calls just didn't do the trick, and the kids increasingly asked him when he was coming down. It was during these times that he sometimes wondered whether having his own business was really worth it. When he was working as the cameraman for the TV station, he always had a full three weeks he could spend on the island with the family, and he was able to go down most weekends. *When you have your own business, you just don't have the same freedom.*

Although he had two reliable clerks for the store in Quincy Market, one full time and the other part time, he still didn't feel comfortable leaving the new business for an extended vacation or for multiple weekends. *Perhaps in a couple of years I'll feel differently, but right now I have to be here.*

He had processed several of the pictures he had taken on the island over the July Fourth holiday, had selected a few that he thought would sell well, and had this week finished the framing. He had already sold a couple of the new lighthouse pictures in Boston, and Amy was anxious for him to bring down some of the prints for the shop in Nantucket. Jack had worked out an arrangement where he had several dozen empty frames shipped directly to the island, so when he went down this weekend, he would carry only the prints and then complete the framing when he arrived. He had set up a small workshop in the cellar of the Nantucket cottage and had enough supplies there that he could do some of the uncomplicated framing.

The word cottage didn't truly describe the Nantucket home since it had a full cellar and was entirely winterized. It was the typical island house style with wood shingle siding and white trim. It was an upside-down house, with the bedrooms on the first floor and the living areas on the second. There were four bedrooms, and for the first time this year both of the children wanted a separate room. Amy's parents had built the house when Amy was an infant, and she had spent time on the island every summer since. Her parents, who were now retired, came to the island only occasionally during the summer, and as an only child Amy would eventually inherit the property. Both she and Jack realized how fortunate they were to have a home on an island where real estate prices had escalated more than in most locations during the previous twenty years.

The second floor of the house had a large open area that had the fairly modern kitchen on one end and a large sitting area with the television at the other. In between was the dining area, which could easily sit eight people. Adjacent to the sitting area was a separate living room with a fireplace and an excellent view looking out to the west toward Madaket. It was the ideal place to catch a good sunset, and there were a multitude of them to choose from on the island during the summer months. Jack had taken hundreds photos of them over the years. By far the best pictures were those where there was either haze or light clouds on the horizon. That combination brought out the most vivid and startling colors. And on the east end of the island in Sconset, the sunrises could also be spectacular. Nantucket was far enough out to sea that Jack could get a view of both the daily coming and the going of the sun over the ocean without the interference of buildings or hills or mountains or trees.

When he was on the island and had a few moments to himself after the kids had gone to bed or were otherwise occupied, he and Amy both enjoyed sitting in the living room reading and inhaling the fresh salt air and listening to the sounds of the island. Even though they were located about a quarter mile from the ocean, they could hear the surf crashing on the beach when the wind was right.

There were other sounds that were unique to the island. The steamship, when it rounded the bend around the Brant Point Lighthouse, would blow its horn announcing its arrival, and of course there was the foghorn's sort of moaning cry warning mariners not only of the shoals surrounding the island, but also of other hazards of sea travel especially within the busy harbor. With almost a constant daily breeze, they could sit in the living room and listen to the soft rustle of the leaves as they brushed each other and brushed against the house. And of course the multitude of seagulls' screeching cries clearly reminded them that they were close to the ocean.

During the winter Jack and Amy would occasionally come to the island to not only check on the property, but also to enjoy the different sounds and sights that come with the changing seasons. Although the temperature on the island is typically ten or more degrees warmer than the mainland, the winter wind blows almost continually and the wind-chill reading and the damp air frequently make it feel as cold as if you were in the New Hampshire mountains. One of the startling sights on a clear fall or winter night is when you can see literally thousands of stars, too many to even think of counting. The clear air away from the air pollution of the mainland always made Jack appreciate how ancient mariners could navigate around the globe. One of his favorite things on such winter visits was to let the children stay up a little later than normal and go out and see the stars. Jack would point out the Big Dipper and the Little Dipper and the North Star. On many nights they were so bright and clear that even the youngest of children could pick them out.

The door to the Quincy Market shop opened, and Jack was shaken out of his daydreaming. He waited while the customer looked around at the various prints on the walls and at the unframed prints in the various containers around the shop. He appeared to be a serious potential purchaser and asked Jack several questions about where and when some of the shots were taken. Finally he settled on buying one of Jack's favorite prints, a picture of the Public Garden right after a snowfall, with the snow still clinging to the trees and before the snow had been disturbed by machinery or footprints.

As the customer left, Jack returned to selecting and packing the prints to take to the island on the weekend. The days just couldn't pass quickly enough for him before he was again with his family, if only for a few days.

Amy left the photo shop on Nantucket and walked to the public parking area to retrieve her car. It was Thursday morning, and Jack would be arriving tomorrow evening for the weekend. It sometimes seemed as though he had been away for months, even though it had been only a couple of weeks. The kids seemed to be missing him more as the summer moved on, especially the roughhousing that only he could do in a way to satisfy the kids. She knew that he missed them and her as much as they missed him, and at times she felt somewhat guilty that he had to carry all of the responsibilities for the Boston business during the summer. But she knew that he would not have it any other way since the time on the island had become such an important part of their life.

She was on her way to a secondhand store on the island to try to find a table to display more of the prints at her store. Jack was bringing down several additional prints, and she was running out of display space. The supply of suitable tables or something else attractive enough to use for showing off the prints was limited in the few retail furniture stores on the island; in addition, she knew that the price of something new would be prohibitive. She was proud of the success of the shop during its first summer and knew that keeping the costs under control was one of the important challenges for any small business.

There were several antique stores on the island that would have all shapes and sizes of tables; however, they tended to be pricey because of the "antique" label, even though it seemed to be a real stretch to call some of the items antiques. The summer seasonal residents and visitors frequented these stores and they were particularly attracted to items that appeared to have some Nantucket connection, almost regardless of the quality of workmanship. A lamp, a chair, an end table, a desk, or a wall hanging that had the image of a whale, a lighthouse, a windmill, or any one of several views of tourist spots on the island were always in demand.

There was, however, one true secondhand store that carried a wide variety of items that did not fall into the antique or unique Nantucket category where Amy hoped she could find what she was looking for. She and Jack had visited the store on several occasions over the years when they were looking for something and didn't want to pay the retail price. Jack in particular had found it a great place to pick up a necessary tool, but inexpensively, for some project that he just didn't have in his limited collection of tools at the summerhouse. They knew that the owner tended to buy up the contents of a house that was being vacated after all of the items that interested the antique dealers had been picked over.

Natalie and Jeremy loved to make the trip to the store since there was usually an ample supply of used children's games and puzzles, and occasionally toys. They could usually find something they "absolutely needed." Even though the summerhouse had enough games and toys to keep the kids occupied, there was simply not the variety of items that they were used to at their home in Quincy. So as Amy walked around the store, she left them to rummage gleefully in the children's area in hopes of finding a true prize.

One of the difficult and sometimes frustrating things about visiting this store was that it was jam packed with narrow aisles and frequently with some items stacked on top of one another. In addition, there seemed to be little logic behind the location of items and how they were displayed. Paintings, prints, rugs, furniture, lamps, beds, bureaus, desks, tables, and kitchen items could be found all over the store, on both floors, with no apparent organization. Amy paused as she started her search and thought *Well, it sure looks disorganized, but maybe the purpose is to get you to move through the whole store in hopes that you'd find something you hadn't planned to buy.* She had been there enough times before to know that the owner seemed to know where everything was, regardless of the seeming gross disorganization.

As she walked among the wide collection of things, many of which she couldn't imagine anyone wanting or needing, it occurred to her that everything in here at some time undoubtedly meant something to someone. There were dozens of tables of every shape, size, color, and design, but she tended to be very picky, especially for an item that was going to be in the store for the public to see.

As she left one aisle and turned into another, she stopped, suddenly noticing a mantel clock set on top of a cupboard. As she studied it further, she realized that it looked exactly like the one that had been stolen from the summerhouse in the spring. She knew that it was not a one-of-a-kind item and that her clock was one of probably hundreds, maybe thousands that had been manufactured.

Still, the coincidence that it was here in this secondhand store made her stop and wonder just where it had come from. She moved on, looking for a table, and after entirely surveying both floors of the store, she thought that there were perhaps two tables that would fit the bill.

She went back to examine those tables more closely and finally decided on one that was in good shape and the right size and color to fit in the store. It was stacked on top of another table, however, so she went to find the owner to help get it down so she could look at it more closely. Tony Andrews was always eager to help and pulled down the table and placed it in an area where Amy could examine it further. She checked it over carefully, especially to see if the legs seemed solid and that there were no ugly marks on the surface. Satisfied, she then asked, "What are you asking for this table?"

Tony looked at the tag that had numbers and letters that meant nothing to Amy but was obviously in some kind of code that Tony understood. He replied, "Well, I've had it listed for one hundred twenty-five dollars, but I can let it go for one ten."

Although Amy knew that it was common to bargain on the price, she really hated this process and wished that Jack was here. He truly enjoyed this game of cat and mouse and always relished saving even a dollar or two. Amy was a little more cynical and was sure that the owner set the initial price high enough that no matter what the lowest offer was that someone made, he would always more than make his margin.

She swallowed and replied, "That's more than what I'd hoped. I was hoping to get what I wanted for around seventy-five dollars."

Tony said, "I couldn't let it go for that price. I paid more than that for it. However, it's been here for a few months, and I've got some new furniture coming in and really need the space. I guess I can let it go for a hundred."

Amy hesitated, knowing Jack would probably at this point still insist on a lower price, but she really wanted the table and had already taken enough time looking for it, so she said, trying to act a little disappointed, "OK, I'll take it for one hundred."

As he was walking away, she said on the spur of the moment, "There's a mantel clock over there I'm interested in, but I can't reach it. Could you help me?"

"Oh sure, I think I know the one you're talking about."

Tony took the clock off the cupboard, handed it to Amy, and then went to take the table out to the front of the store. Amy looked the clock over carefully, and the more she examined it the more she was certain that it looked exactly like the one that had been stolen. As she turned it over on the back, she noticed that the metal plate covering the inside works was held on by four screws, but one of the screws was a different style. She remembered that she had taken off the back plate a couple of years ago and replaced a battery but couldn't find the fourth screw when she was reassembling it. She recalled how difficult it had been for her to rummage through a can of odd screws that Jack kept in the cellar until she found one that was the right size to fit in the hole. She was convinced that this was the same clock.

Tony came back to see whether or not he had made another sale, and Amy thought quickly to herself, *What am I going to do? If this is my clock, I want it back, but I don't want to accuse this guy of dealing in stolen property. But I'm sure as heck not going to buy back my own clock.*

She decided to play along a little and said, "Well, how much is it?"

Tony went through the same process of looking at the tag on the clock and said, "I'm asking sixty dollars. You know these things go for around two hundred new, and this one is in really good shape."

Pushing further and a little angry at this point, Amy said, "You know, I had one like this in my home here on island, but we had a break-in last winter and it was stolen along with a lot of other things. Do you know where this one came from?"

Tony, truly alarmed, hesitated as he looked at Amy and replied, "You know, I really can't remember. There's so much stuff in here that I can't keep track of all of it. It's a fairly common style of clock, and I'm sure it came from some house where I had bought out all of the contents."

And then trying to cover up further, he said, "I'm sure it's been here for a couple of years."

Amy said, "Oh, well I'm really not interested in buying it. But it certainly looks identical to the one I had."

She abruptly moved away from the area and went to retrieve her children and whatever "absolutely necessary" things they had discovered.

The table was loaded into the car, along with a couple of puzzles for the kids, and as Amy drove back to the store she thought, *I'm positive that clock is ours. Although I didn't see anything as I was walking around, I wonder if any of our other stuff is there somewhere. Come to think of it, I really didn't see much electronic equipment or TVs. The owner seemed to be uneasy when I mentioned that it looked like mine, and his explanation just doesn't make sense. There just aren't two of the same clocks with one odd screw on the back. I've got to tell Jack and see what he thinks we should do.*

July 2009

It was one of those beautiful summer weekends on Nantucket, and the crowds at all of the beaches made it difficult to find a place to plant an umbrella and set up beach chairs. At Surfside Beach, one of the most popular beaches on the island, children were enjoying playing in the sand but especially frolicking in the surf, daring the waves to catch them and knock them off their feet. Some days the surf was so high and forceful that younger children stayed only on the edge of the water and left the teenagers to be wrestled to the ground. On occasion with the high surf beachgoers had to be on the lookout for riptides, and the warning signs were clearly placed up and down the beach area as to the danger. This was one of the beaches where the lifeguards had to be continually alert for swimmers who misjudged the power of waves, and it was not unusual to see them quickly go into the surf with one of their rescue buoys or a surfboard to help someone in trouble.

Dick Gimble and Allison sat on the beach, enjoying the sun and watching others in the surf. When they first arrived, Dick had briefly gone into the water, but Allison had elected to stay sunning on the beach, still a little apprehensive about doing anything that might bring back any of the symptoms of her injuries.

Dick had called her last week and told her he was coming to Nantucket to visit an old college roommate and would like to get together with her. She was somewhat flattered that he was interested in seeing her again, and she had looked forward to the weekend. He met Jack when he picked Allison up at the summerhouse, and they had spent several hours in the sun. As they sat on the beach, Dick talked and laughed about some of his college experiences with Tony Andrews, but he never mentioned Tony's involvement with drugs. He told Allison about his one visit to the island several years ago when he was in college and how the island had changed, and he subtly let her know that his only reason for coming to the island now was to see her. They had biked out to the beach and planned to get a late lunch and then spend the afternoon together doing some sightseeing.

Something Natural was a favorite spot for takeout sandwiches and salads about a half mile out of town on Cliff Road. A full sandwich was enormous, twice the size of a normal sandwich because the bread loaf was cut the long way, and most visitors could not escape without buying at least one oatmeal raisin cookie. Allison had a salad while Dick devoured a roast beef sandwich along with a couple of bags of potato chips. After lunch they got back on their bikes and rode the five miles out to village of Madaket on the west corner of the island. There was a well-used bike bath for almost the entire distance, which made the ride especially relaxing and enjoyable.

It was obvious to Dick that Allison was getting back into her riding form, and he found he had to struggle a little to keep up with her pace, particularly on the several hills as they wound through the low brush. Allison said that this was a ride she took almost every morning, and she found it invigorating to get out just after sunrise before anyone else was on the bike path.

They grabbed a couple of towels after reaching the end of Madaket Road and sat on the beach again to simply enjoy the scenery before heading back into town. They talked about her injuries, and Allison enthusiastically said how great she felt and how the time on Nantucket truly seemed to have brought her over the last hurdles in her recovery. She felt stronger, had gotten a lot of good exercise, and was looking forward to getting back to work. Her headaches had disappeared almost entirely, and she mentioned that she had even begun to get back into the actuarial studies that she had been working on before the accident.

Dick perked up at her mention of the studies and, trying carefully not to appear too interested, innocently asked her, "What studies are you talking about?"

Allison replied, "Well, it's one I know I mentioned to you that I was working on before I was injured. It's a study that involves accident claims in the Northeast. I just sort of stumbled across some abnormalities when I was doing some routine year-end studies about a year ago."

"Oh yeah, I do remember now your saying something about it."

"It's one of those things that's really been bugging me because I haven't been able to come up with any logical explanation for the increase in these accident claims. It doesn't amount to millions of dollars of losses, so I've had a hard time getting my manager to take the study seriously."

Dick didn't answer right away. He was engrossed in what she was saying and could feel alarm bells going off in his head. He had to learn more, but he had to be extremely careful that she didn't become too suspicious of his interest. He tried to be as casual as possible and asked, "What do you mean he doesn't take you seriously?"

"Oh, I didn't mean that he doesn't take me seriously. He and I really have a good relationship, and I know he respects my opinions. It's just that he looks at this study as not that important in the larger scheme of things. But I'm now at a point where I just can't let it go."

Dick, a little too quickly, asked, "What do you mean?"

"Well, I've spent enough time looking at the data on the claims and there are just too many coincidences that don't make sense."

Dick couldn't help but show his continued interest and again quickly asked, "What kind of coincidences?"

"Do you really want me to get into the boring details of an actuarial study? You know how pedantic we are."

"Hey, I'm a claim examiner, and I'm really interested." And then, on the spur of the moment he said, "Maybe I can help you solve the puzzle."

"Well, maybe you can help me figure this out. Let me give you a little of the background."

Allison then described what she had found, the similarities in the types of claims, the size of each policy, the length of the claims, the fact that they were all in the Northeast, and that they all lapsed a short time after the claim ended. She ended by saying, "I estimate that the claim loss is about one hundred thousand dollars a year, and that adds up to almost a half million over the past five years. I know it's not millions, but something's not right."

Dick hesitatingly replied, "Yeah, I can see where that's something you just can't ignore. Well, what do you think's going on?"

"Well, initially I wondered if the underwriters were sloppy and missing some important health history in underwriting the applications, but all the claims are accidental, so that really doesn't make much sense. I think there's some kind of fraud involved. Somebody's trying to rip off the company. I just can't figure out how it's being done."

Trying to act still interested but a little naïve, Dick asked, "Do you think it's some kind of a fraud ring of policyholders or some agent that's behind it?"

"Well, I know it's not an agent because all of the policies were bought directly over the Internet with no agent involved. Someone, either inside or outside the company, has found some loopholes in our systems, some weak spots in our procedures. Maybe that's where you can help me out."

"How many claims are we talking about?"

"Well, over the past five years it's been about two hundred, about fifty a year."

Dick had never added up the total claims involved, but he knew this sounded pretty close to the number. "Wow! It doesn't seem possible that that many phony claims could get by the claim department."

"Yeah, except that none of them were large claims, and they all ended after a few weeks, so I guess they didn't require investigation."

"What else have you learned?"

"Well, I've sort of gone as far as I can go with the data that's available to me here, but I'm now going to look at the applications and some of the claim files in more detail. The apps are all electronic, so I can access them from my computer, but the claims are all hard copy, so someone has to pull them."

Dick realized that this whole investigation was now getting out of hand, and the odds of Allison finding out something that would lead her back to Ed and him were increasing dramatically. "Are they going to send the claims to you down here?"

"Well, I can download the apps here and see if anything jumps out at me, but I've probably got to wait until I'm back at work to look at the claims."

At this point Dick did not want to ask any more questions; he just wanted to get away from Allison and think about whether there was anything he could do to stop her investigation. On the spur of the moment he said, "I don't know what to say except maybe I could look at the claims and pick out something."

Allison said, "Let me get back to work and then maybe I can use your help."

"OK. I think it's time we headed back to town."

"Sure, and incidentally I'd appreciate your not mentioning this to anyone since we don't know who may be behind it."

"Yeah, I understand."

Dick had spent the reminder of the day becoming more and more anxious, so by the time he sat down with Tony later that evening, he was visibly shaken.

Tony kidded him and said, "What's the matter? Wasn't your girl everything you hoped for? No action, Dick?"

Dick, not really wanting to talk about the day with Allison, said, "Yeah, something like that. What I really need are a couple of stiff drinks."

Tony stared at Dick. He'd never heard him ask for hard liquor. He'd always been a beer-only man in college, even when everyone else was experimenting with the hard stuff. Things must really be bad. "OK. What do you want?"

"I don't know—how about some bourbon on the rocks? If you don't have any bourbon, then any whisky'll do."

"I think I've got some Jim Beam."

A couple of hours later both Dick and Tony had downed several drinks and had clearly reached that point where they had become tipsy, their thinking a little clouded, and their tongues had become a little loose. Tony began to complain about the pressures of his business.

Dick, his speech definitely very thick, said, "Oh, come on, Tony. You've got a great setup here. Your business is booming. Looks to me like you haven't got a care in the world." After a pause he continued, "I wish I had your problems."

"Things aren't always the way they look, Dick. This island may look like paradise, but I've got some real problems."

"Don't talk to me about problems. I've got my own."

They each filled up their glasses again, and Tony then mentioned that the police were conducting an investigation on drug trafficking on the island.

Dick said, "Don't tell me you're still dealing, Tony."

Tony hesitated, realizing he had brought up a dangerous subject, but then he remembered that Dick was aware of his college activities. "Well, just a little with close friends."

"Are the police after you?"

"No, I don't think so. I've been very careful. I'm a friend of the police inspector who came around last week. He sort of wanted my thoughts on what I might have heard since I'm pretty well plugged-in on the island." He mumbled again hopefully, "No, I don't think anyone suspects."

"Jesus. You'd better be careful."

"Yeah, so what's your problem?'

Dick stared at his glass of liquor, remembering the disturbing conversation with Allison, and said, "Oh, it's nothing you'd be interested in."

Tony, with a liquor-thickened voice, said, "Hey, we've been friends for a long time. I've leveled with you. So you've got girl problems. You're not the first one."

"It's more than that, Tony." Dick then began to tell Tony about the claim scheme. He started out describing it as sort of a game he was playing, trying to test the company's systems. But as he rambled on more through the alcoholic haze, he went further into the entire claim fraud scheme, and finally he even told Tony about having forced Allison off the road.

After listening to Dick, Tony said, "Wow. You really do have a problem. So what are you gonna do now?"

"I don't know. Somehow I've got to stop this fucking investigation from going any further."

"How the hell are you going to do that?"

"I really don't know. This girl seems hell-bent on going ahead with the goddamn study even though her boss doesn't seem very interested. If I could find a way of stopping her, then I don't think the company would keep it going."

"How can you stop her?"

"Shit, I don't know. I tried that once, but that didn't work."

"Christ, you're really up against it. Maybe she's just gotta have another accident."

"Tony, I took a real risk the first time. I don't think I can chance it again."

Trying to clear his thinking, Tony said, "Maybe you should get someone else to really pull it off this time." Jokingly, he said, "I've got some real nasty characters down here. For a few bucks they'd do anything to be able to get their next fix."

"Oh sure, that's all I need to do now is get involved with some druggies."

"Hey, don't pass it off so quickly. You're in a real bind. You've gotta do something. You can't just let this thing blow up and hang you."

July 2009

The next morning was a Sunday, and Dick was packing his bag to return to the mainland. He felt considerably hungover from the previous evening, but that was minimal in comparison to the depression over how was he going to stop Allison from continuing on with her investigation.

Both he and Tony were unusually quiet as they sat down at the breakfast table. Tony wasn't much of a cook and usually got his meals on the fly, and they were typically high in calories and cholesterol. He had downed three large sticky buns, along with two cups of coffee, heavily laden with cream and sugar. Dick was poking at a bowl of dry cereal.

Finally Tony broke the silence and said, "I've been thinking about our conversation last night, about both of our problems. I think there may be a way we can help each other."

Dick looked at him, not really focusing on what Tony had said, and replied, "Sure, what are you gonna do, offer me a job?"

"Look, I'm serious. One of my problems is that I've been taking in a large amount of cash in my business, and to be honest with you, most of it is from the drugs. I'm into this a little deeper than I told you last night. The immediate problem is that I can't deposit it all in an on-island bank, especially now with this investigation going on. Someone may get suspicious that the size of the deposits just won't jibe with my secondhand business. In the winter and spring I can get off island every couple of weeks and I can deposit money in three of four different accounts I have on the mainland, but things are so busy in the summer that I can't take the time to leave here."

Dick, beginning to pay attention to Tony's words, said, "Yeah, so you got too much money and don't know what to do with it. I wish I had your problem."

"Look, I've got more than a hundred thousand dollars in the safe upstairs that I've been collecting over the past two months, and more is coming in every day. I don't want all that cash sitting around." He looked at Dick to make sure he was taking him seriously, and then went on. "If you'll take that money with you when you leave and deposit it for me, then maybe I can arrange to do something in return."

Now he had Dick's full attention, and Dick stared at him intently and said, "What are you talking about?"

Tony looked directly at him and said, "If you'll take the money and deposit it, then I think I can arrange for your girlfriend have another accident."

Dick, not really believing that any plan that Tony had thought up would solve his problem, said, "What the hell are you talking about?"

"Last night you mentioned that this girl was a real exercise fiend and has been going for a bike ride out to Madaket real early every morning."

"Yeah."

"Well, supposing I could arrange for someone to stage another accident, but this time make it stick?"

Dick hardly hesitated a second after fully grasping what was being offered and replied, "Tell me more."

"I told you that I'm dealing with some guys who are desperate for their drugs, and some of them I know wouldn't hesitate to do just about anything for the right sum of money."

Dick, playing along but still not fully buying it, said, "How much are you talking about?"

"Look, I think if I offered five thousand dollars to the guy I have in mind that he'd jump at it."

"I don't know, it sounds to me like a lot could go wrong, and I'll be in deeper than I am right now."

"Look, Dick, why don't you think it over, but in the meantime will you take this money with you today and deposit it?"

"Yeah, I guess I can do that. But I'm not ready to do anything else right now."

"OK, I hear you, but you know you can give me a call at any time."

"Sure—and thanks."

July 2009

When Jack had arrived on the island on this weekend, late in July, Amy had told him about the mantle clock she had seen at the secondhand store. At first he thought she was overreacting, but as she further described the clock and especially the fact that the screws were different, just like the one they had, Jack began to believe she was on to something.

The next morning Jack had gone out to the store by himself to look at the clock. Amy had described in detail where it was located, and he was certain that if he looked it over he'd be able to tell whether it was the one where they had replaced the screw. However, when he found the cupboard where she had said the clock was located, it wasn't there. He spent several minutes looking around the store to see if it was in another location, but he couldn't locate it.

Finally he had walked over to the person behind a desk that he assumed was the owner of the store and said, "I'm looking for a clock that my wife saw in here a few days ago. She wants me to take a look at it before we make an offer. It was a mantel clock, and she said it was over there, on that cupboard."

Tony looked up at Jack and, after thinking for a few seconds, replied, "Oh yeah, I remember your wife. She bought a table from me that day. I do remember the clock you're talking about, but I'm afraid that I sold it yesterday."

Tony had actually removed the clock from the store immediately after Amy had left, sensing that her interest was more than what she had indicated. "Look, I do have a few more mantel clocks that you might be interested in."

Jack looked at Tony, trying to sense if there was truth in what he was saying, and replied, "No, my wife was really set on that one. Do you know who bought it from you?"

Tony quickly replied, "No, it was a cash sale, and I'm sure I didn't keep any record of the buyer. It wasn't anyone local. We sell a lot to visitors and summer residents during this time of year. Sorry I can't help you out there."

Jack left the store at that point and on the way back to their summer home decided to place a call to Detective Collins. Collins, after making sure that Jack knew he was very busy, agreed to meet with him that afternoon. Jack was somewhat surprised that he had agreed to see him so soon since their relationship in the past had been strained, going back to his contact with Collins a few years previously when Jack had inadvertently been a witness in a drug-related investigation.

After exchanging pleasantries with the detective, Jack told him about Amy's visit to the secondhand store and the clock she'd found that she was certain was the one stolen from their house.

Al listened to Jack explain about his own visit to the store that morning and what the owner had told him about the clock having been sold. Jack said, "Kind of convenient for the clock to have been sold, don't you think? Amy and I think this guy Andrews may have gotten suspicious when Amy told him the clock was just like the one that had been stolen."

Al looked at Jack and said, "Well, let's not jump to conclusions. First of all, from what you say, you can't be absolutely sure it was the same clock. Secondly, I know Tony Andrews pretty well, and I'm certain he wouldn't knowingly deal in stolen property.

And thirdly, without the clock to examine we really don't have anywhere else to go. Did you ask him where he got the clock?"

"My wife did, and he told her he thought he got it a couple of years ago along with the contents of a house he'd bought," Jack said. "And then, after sitting around in that store for two years, it's sold right after Amy was there. It sure sounds pretty unlikely to me."

"Look, Mr. Kendrick, coincidences happen all the time. I really don't have anything solid to take this any further."

Jack replied, "Well, my wife was pretty certain it was our clock because of the screw being replaced on the back. It's not the value of the clock I'm concerned about, but rather if we could find where this guy Tony got it, then it might lead us to the person who broke into our house and stole all of the electronic equipment. That's what I'm really interested in."

Al, irritated that Jack was trying to do his job, said, "I think you're leaping into this way too far. We haven't got the clock, and you don't even know that it was the one stolen from you house anyway."

Jack, sensing Al's irritation, tried to play up to his ego and said, "I know it may be a long shot, but I thought if you went to see the owner yourself he might be more forthcoming to the police than to me, especially if he's someone that you know. Maybe he'll remember just where he got the clock."

Al stood up from behind his desk, anxious to end the conversation, but wanting to humor Jack a little, and said, "Well, let me think about it. I may go out and have a chat with Tony. Thanks for coming in, and I want to assure you that we're still working hard on trying to solve your break-in."

Jack realized that he was being rushed out of the interview, but knowing he couldn't push Al any further, he said, "Thanks, and please let me know if you find out anything more. I'll be here over the weekend, but my wife will be on island for the rest of the summer."

July 2009

Dick Gimble was sitting with Ed Fletcher at lunch. Ed had called him and said he had some more information concerning the claim investigation and needed to talk with him. Dick had returned from the island, taken off a half day from work, and had made the deposits for Tony in three different banks in the Boston area. He had called Tony and told him the money was in the banks, and Tony again reminded him, "I can still help you out with your problem. Give me a call if you want me to look into it, and many thanks for making the deposits. It's a big load off my mind."

Ed explained to Dick that he had overheard a couple of actuaries saying that Allison would be returning to work in September. Furthermore, he heard one of them say that she had been working on the claim study while she was on vacation. One of them had sort of indicated that she was consumed with this study even though it wasn't one of the more important things in their boss's mind.

Dick had deliberately kept Ed in the dark about his visit to Nantucket and didn't want to involve Ed any further with the claim scheme problem. He just didn't trust Ed to remain cool if he knew all that was going on. He was just too much on edge, and Dick feared that Ed could inadvertently say something, or worse still, he might decide to go to management and confess everything. He thought, *I really made a mistake in involving him in the first place. I could have pulled it all off on my own, and I would have been a lot better off financially.*

Dick felt it was best to continue to downplay the problem and decided to deliberately understate his own fears. "Well I've seen Allison a couple of times since we last talked, and I don't really think we have anything to worry about." He then sort of casually asked, "What exactly did these actuaries say about the claim study?"

"Nothing more than what I said, but it sure sounds like she's ready to seriously get back into it. I can't stand all this tension, Dick."

"Look, I said there's nothing to worry about. They were probably talking about a different study altogether."

"I don't think so."

"Relax, Ed. Let me know if you hear anything more, and I'll do the same."

"OK, Dick, but I've got to tell you that I'm not sleeping very well, and I'm scared to death they're going to trace this to us even though it's been almost a year since we stopped. I wish like hell we'd never started."

"Well, we did and nothing's happened so far, so keep cool."

Dick left and decided he'd give Allison a call that night to try to find out if she had found out anything more in her investigation.

When he got back to his apartment, Dick placed the call to Allison, and after talking a little about the day they had spent together on Nantucket, he decided to take the risk of showing too much interest and said, "You know, I've been thinking about your claim study, and I think I might be able to help out."

Allison said, "What do you mean?"

"Well, you said you were going to pull out some claim files and see what you could find. I know my way around those files as well as anyone, and I might be able to see something that someone who's not an examiner might miss."

He thought that if he could keep her away from examining the files herself, then at least there wouldn't be the risk of her picking up any more inconsistencies.

Allison was somewhat intrigued with Dick's offer and said, "Gee, that might be a big help, especially since the files are at the home office and I won't be able to look at them until I get back to work. But you know, I've come across something else since I saw you."

Dick quickly asked, "What's that?"

"I told you that I was going to look at some of the application detail, and I've been doing that over the past few days. Well, I downloaded some thirty or forty apps that are in my study, and I noticed that although the street addresses are all different, all of them list the same post office box number. It's not a regular U.S. post office box, but rather it's with one of those private companies that do packaging and mailing and also have private boxes for mail. I think they're called PMBs for personal mailbox, or something like that. In addition, I've checked out a few of the actual street addresses on the apps, and they're all phony ones. They just don't exist."

Dick's hand holding the phone was trembling, and he almost dropped it on the floor. This was one area in his scheme that he had always most feared. "Wow, that sure sounds fishy, but I can't believe that somewhere along the way someone wouldn't have picked it up."

"You remember, I told you that everything about these apps was done electronically? There was no agent involved, the apps were completed through the company's online Web site, and the premiums were all paid electronically. There's been no normal underwriting investigation as near as I can tell, and any screening was done within the computer program, and so no one checked out street addresses. The only things that went through the regular mail were the final policy contracts, and they all would have gone to this private box number."

Dick, trying to recover from his shock, said, "Well, where do you go from here?" And then, concerned about who else she had talked to, he added, "What does your boss say about it?"

"I haven't talked to anyone else about this yet. I'm trying to figure out what the next step should be. My boss hasn't been very supportive, and I want to make sure of my facts before I approach him again."

Trying to sound helpful and learn more, Dick said, "Well, it sure sounds like you've stumbled on something really important. Where's this mailbox located?"

"It's out in Natick. I don't have the exact address, but it's somewhere on Route 9. It's one of those private packaging companies called Pack and Post. Have you ever used one for packaging?"

"No."

"Well, it's a business that's grown up in the past ten years or so, and it's pretty convenient. You just bring in something you want wrapped and mailed, and they do the whole thing for you. In addition, they have on the wall fifty or so mailboxes that look like the kind you see in the post office. Some people and businesses prefer to rent them and have their regular mail come there, primarily because the hours are more convenient than the U.S. post office."

At this point Dick had heard enough and needed to end the conversation. "You've certainly made some real headway. Look, I've got to go right now, but let me know if I can help you out by looking at the claim files."

Allison was a little surprised by the quick end to the conversation, but she replied, "OK, let me think about it."

July 2009

After Dick ended the telephone call with Allison, he hesitated for only a couple of minutes and then placed a call to Tony Andrews.

"Hi, Tony, it's Dick. How's it goin'?"

"Oh, about the same, Dick. What's up with you?"

"Well, I've been thinking about our conversation about my problem, and I'd like to talk about it further."

"Has something else happened?"

"Yeah, I'm really convinced she's getting a lot closer to figuring it out."

"OK. You know, I did offer to help out, and that still goes."

Dick said, "Yeah, I really appreciate it, but I need some more details. How much is it going to cost me?" There was then a pause in the conversation before he continued, "And how and when would you do it?"

"I think I told you that I'm pretty sure we can do it for around five grand. Can you handle that?"

Dick quickly replied, "It's a stretch, but I can swing it. I don't have any damn choice. But when and how do you want the money?"

"I don't want it by check. Cash is the only way to handle it. I can take care of it from my end, and then you can pay me later. Let's talk about some of the other details I need to know."

"OK."

"I've got a guy who I'm pretty sure will jump at the chance for five grand. As a matter of fact, he's in hock to me right now, and every week he's having trouble coming up with enough cash to keep his habit going. But I need to set things up for him. You mentioned that this person we're talking about takes a bike ride every morning, early."

"Yeah, that's right. She's a real bike nut and tells me she gets out on the Madaket bike path every morning by six o'clock. She gets on where the path starts on Madaket Road and rides the five miles out to the end and then back."

"Well, that's probably the place to arrange it. Are you sure she does this every day?"

"Yeah, that's what she said, and she's really an exercise freak."

"How about the time? How sure are you that it's around six o'clock?"

"Again, that's what she told me, Tony."

"OK, we'll have to check on that. I'll probably take a ride out there myself on a couple of mornings to see if I can locate her. Let me talk with this guy and see if I can put it together."

Dick was perspiring so profusely that the phone was slipping in his hand, but he needed to know a little more. "OK, Tony, and thanks." He paused continued and asked, "When do you think you might be able to pull this off?"

"Well, I know you've got a big problem, so the sooner the better! Oh, one other thing. Can you send me a picture of her?"

Dick considered his reply and said, "Yeah, I think I can get one at the company."

"Why don't you send it to me by overnight mail?"

"I'll try to take care of it tomorrow."

"Good, I'll call you back in the next day or two once I've talked to this guy and I've got the picture."

It was the first day of August, and with each passing week, Allison was feeling stronger and more anxious to get back to the office and her regular routine. The weeks with Amy and her family had been great for her recuperation, but now she was getting impatient to get on with her life.

As she dressed in her biker gear, she looked forward to the forty-minute bike ride that had become a part of her morning routine. She had entered the Madaket bike path where it began, about a mile out of town, but only a few hundred yards from Amy and Jack's summer home. It was a misty morning with the thick fog hanging low over the island. The flights to and from Hyannis and Boston would surely be delayed for a couple of hours, and the

Boston newspapers wouldn't be on the shelves until late morning. The papers usually came over by plane around six o'clock so that those anxious to get caught up on yesterday's news could have the paper with their morning coffee. But today, it would be a news-free cup, perhaps a chance to enjoy the sounds and smells of the island.

Allison cruised along the path, mostly free of joggers, walkers, and other bikers at this early hour. It felt so good to have her body finally responding effortlessly to the small hills as she wound her way toward Madaket. Even the mist from the fog increased her feeling of exhilaration as she gradually picked up her speed to more than fifteen miles per hour. She let her mind wander over her plans for the next few weeks before she returned to work. Although she missed the routine of work, her friends at work, and the commitment to her actuarial studies, she also had to admit that the past several months of recuperation had given her a unique opportunity to rethink her future. She still remained committed to completing her actuarial exams and attaining her fellowship designation, but she also came to think more about her biological clock and what else she wanted in her life. After spending several weeks with Amy and her children, the thought of beginning her own family seemed to take on more importance in her plans.

She had never had a truly serious relationship and, in fact, had not had many dates in the few years she had worked at the insurance company. Her recent meetings and dates with Dick Gimble represented by far the most contact she'd had with any male since college. She was intrigued by his attention to her, but she was not at a point where it had graduated to a romantic interest. The fact that he was recently divorced continued to be a concern to her, but perhaps more important was her feeling that something about him made her uneasy. *He's not a naturally open person. I just don't know what he's really thinking a lot of the time. I often think he just sort of says what he thinks I want to hear. He seems to be interested in me, but I don't know if I want it to go any further. Well, it's been fun to have some attention.*

She had passed Cliff Road and the water tower, and as she rode at an even a faster clip, she approached and area on the bike path where it moved several yards away from the main road. As she rounded a bend, secluded now from the road and any passing motorists, she suddenly came upon a deer foraging at the side of the path. The startled animal turned quickly and leaped down the path to escape the strange, brightly colored object coming toward it. At the same time as Allison was slowing the bike to allow the deer to get away, the animal, as it leaped, was suddenly thrown violently into the air and fell into a heap on the asphalt path.

Allison immediately began to brake her bike, but as she approached the deer, the bike struck a wire that was stretched across the path. And although she had slowed considerably, the impact threw her off the bike, and her leg struck the wire as she was also thrown into the air.

The deer was badly injured and bleeding, and at least one of its front legs appeared to be broken. It was making weird whimpering noises and trying to drag itself off of the path and into the brush, away from this strange vehicle that had landed only a few feet away.

Allison was stunned, but not unconscious. Her first thought was, *How could this be happening to me again?* Her shirt was torn on the sleeve where she had tried to break her fall, and her elbow was badly skinned. More importantly, the leg that had struck the wire was severely cut and bleeding. She looked around and noticed the wire both she and the unfortunate animal had hit. It was strung tightly been two small trees about two feet off the ground.

After a few moments she sat up, and noticing the severity of her leg wound, she tried to apply pressure to slow down the bleeding. At the same time the frightened deer had successfully dragged itself into the bushes. Allison, however, was unsuccessful in stemming the bleeding and finally pulled a shoestring from one of her sneakers and tied it as a tourniquet around her leg. She thought about getting back on the bike, but she noticed that the front tire had been flattened, and in any event, she realized she was not in any condition to ride.

She stood up, somewhat wobbly, and hobbled through the bushes to the main road. Only a few minutes passed before she was able to wave down a passing motorist, and after explaining what had happened, she asked him to call the police. By this time the bleeding in her leg had slowed considerably, but she could see that the size of the wound would require stitches.

Some distance away on a narrow dirt drive, a man sat in his car observing all the events. He swore to himself as he saw the accident unfold and cursed at his misfortune that the deer had truly messed up his plan. He had waited for about a half hour after stretching the wire across the path, and he had expected that the rider's injuries at her speed of almost twenty miles per hour would have been truly severe and hopefully even fatal. He had even been prepared to finish off the rider with a couple of blows to the head, but the fully conscious victim made that too complicated. He had left after he saw her get to her feet and wave down the motorist.

The police and an ambulance arrived after only a few minutes and gave immediate first aid to Allison. They removed the wire, and a police detective found the deer nearby in the bushes. By this time its loss of blood had brought the animal close to death, and one of the detectives took his pistol and put it out of its misery.

They took a statement from Allison after she was transported to the hospital by ambulance. A doctor examined her thoroughly and cleaned the wound, closing it with thirteen stitches. The police told her that it appeared to be a teenage prank and that they'd look around the scene for any evidence.

She had called Amy from the hospital and explained the events of the early morning. As she rested on a sofa at the summerhouse, still shaken from the experience, her thoughts and plans for the future had been pushed to the recesses of her mind. She found herself reliving the injuries of a year before and wondering, *How can this be happening again?*

40

August 2009

Jack Kendrick had not planned to be back on the island this weekend in early August, but when Amy called on Thursday and told
him about Allison's accident, he rearranged his weekend plans. Amy
had said that Allison was really upset and would be on crutches
for a few days because of the injury to her leg. The injury was also
going to delay her leaving the island and perhaps even when she
planned to return to work.

Jack arrived on Nantucket on Friday evening, and after the
nightly routine of putting the kids to bed, he sat down with
Allison to hear the details of the accident. The more he learned
the more unusual the circumstances sounded. Being an avid reader

of mysteries, his creative imagination began to explore all sorts of possibilities and conspiracies.

"Allison, you're so lucky you weren't injured more seriously. If you'd hit that wire at a higher speed, it could have been fatal."

"I know, and I lay awake at night thinking about it. I can't imagine the kind of person who would think that putting a wire across that path was an innocent prank."

Jack replied, "Yeah, I know. Anyone who lives around here knows that that bike path gets a lot of use, and most bikers are going along at a pretty good clip, although nowhere near as fast as you do."

"I talked with the police again yesterday, some detective named Collins, and he said he was quite sure it was some young kids out, in his words, 'raising hell,' who stretched the wire the night before."

"Yeah, I know Collins. The thing that doesn't make sense is that some kids would put the wire there at a time when they wouldn't see the results. Usually kids want to stay around and see how their prank worked out. Putting it there the night before just doesn't make a lot of sense to me."

"Jack, they also said they looked around the area for any evidence they could find to identify who was there, but there was nothing. The only thing he said to me before he hung up was they'd do some checking around town and see if anyone knew anything. He said sometimes kids brag about what they've done."

"Well, my experience with Collins going back to the terrorist incident a few years ago is that he doesn't really push to get to the bottom of things. I talked to him about our break-in over the winter, and I got the feeling he really didn't want to be bothered."

"That really doesn't make me feel any better."

After a pause, Jack said, "Look, will you drive out to the bike path with me tomorrow and show me where it happened?"

"Yeah, I suppose so, but what do you expect to find?"

"Well, you know me. I'm just curious."

Early on Saturday morning, Jack and Allison drove the two miles out to the site of the accident. Allison, still on crutches, stayed in the car after pointing out to Jack the place on the bike path where the wire had been. Jack found the two trees where the wire had been attached, and the grooves in the trees made them quite easy to identify. He had brought one of his cameras along, just from force of habit, and he took photos of both trees. He spent some time looking around the area further and thought he could identify where the deer had dragged itself because there was a large area in the low bushes that was matted down and stained much darker than the ground around it.

After circling the area several times looking around for anything that the police might have missed, he absentmindedly picked up a small piece of blank paper that was under a bush near one of the trees. As he picked it up, he realized it was a pocket-sized photo, and as he turned it over, he noticed that it was a picture of a person. He wiped off the moisture and some dirt that had accumulated on the photo, and he was startled to see that it was a picture of Allison. *Why would she be carrying a photo of herself on a bike ride?*

He looked around a little more and then returned to the car. As he settled behind the wheel, he handed the photo to Allison and said, "I found this by one of the trees. You must have lost it at the time of the accident."

Allison looked at the picture, completely confused and startled, and said, "I didn't drop it!"

"What do you mean? It's a picture of you!"

"I know, Jack, but I don't carry a picture of myself around. It looks like one of the company photos they took for their records when I was hired. You know, it's the one they keep on file and use in the company newsletter."

"Well, how the hell did it get here?"

"I don't have any idea at all."

They both sat there quietly for a while, and then Jack started up the car and drove back to the summerhouse. Back at the house, Jack said, "Something sure isn't right. I think I'll take this down to the police station and tell them where we found it."

Jack had already in his mind concluded that the existence of the photo seemed to indicate that the wire across the path was deliberately intended to injure Allison. But beyond that he could make no sense out of it. He didn't want to bring this possibility up to Allison right away because the implications would certainly frighten her. He thought that at least the police would now take this more seriously.

Dick Gimble again sat alone in his small apartment with a half-open bottle of whiskey on the floor beside his chair. He filled his glass for the third time in a half hour, not bothering to get ice as he had done for the first drink. Although his mind had not yet become clouded, he knew that would follow shortly; he looked ahead, anticipating and welcoming that moment.

When he had arrived home that Friday evening, there was a message from Tony Andrews on his answering machine. He anxiously dialed Tony's number, anticipating that the accident had been arranged and hoping that his problem was finally solved, but the news could not have been worse. A goddamn deer had screwed up the plan, and Allison apparently had only minor injuries.

He asked Tony, "Was the guy you hired seen by anyone?"

"He said that he wasn't. He stayed well out of sight and left before any of the police arrived."

"I sure hope he's leveling with you. What a goddamn botched-up mess!"

"Yeah, look, Dick, I'm sorry it didn't work out, but I don't think there's anything more I can do right now."

"I'm not paying this stupid bastard anything."

"Dick, it's really not his fault. But I did tell him that he wouldn't get anything."

As Dick angrily hung up the phone, he said, "Well, at least I'm not having to lay out any bucks. That's one small plus."

Dick continued to ruminate about his serious predicament and became increasingly alarmed and frightened even as his mind became more and more clouded from the alcohol. *What in God's name am I going to do? I know she's getting close to finding me out, and I know she's so goddamn persistent that nothing is going to stop her from continuing the study.*

As he took another large swallow of the soothing whiskey, his mind began to play spasmodically with other options. *Maybe I could arrange something that looks like a suicide, like carbon monoxide, or an overdose of drugs. There's no way I can try another bike accident. Maybe there's a way of coming up with some kind of poison that would work. If I was on Nantucket, I might be able to arrange a drowning accident. Shit, what a mess! And anything I try now will be an even bigger goddamn risk.* He had previously considered several ways he might be able to discredit her work at the office and get her fired, or at least moved out of the disability department, but he couldn't come up with any reasonable scenario that would make sense. For some time he kept coming back to all of the possibilities, but with each sip of the liquor his thought process became less and less focused.

Finally, after still another stiff drink, he fell into a fitful slumber.

42

August 2009

Jack was driving back to his summerhouse after having visited with Al Collins at the police department. He could sense when he first placed the telephone call to Collins that the detective really didn't want to spend any time listening to him again; however, he reluctantly agreed.

Jack told Collins where he had found the photo of Allison and that she had assured him it had not been in her possession. He told him she thought it was a company photo, and Jack then asked Collins if they could check it for fingerprints. After looking over the photo, Collins said it would be difficult since it had been handled by several people and had been out in the weather for a few days. But he said, "I'll run it through the process, but don't get your hopes up."

Jack then told Collins about Allison's previous accident and her injuries almost twelve months before. He said, "I'm beginning to think these two incidents are connected and were a deliberate attempt to either injure her or worse. As a matter of fact, she almost died from the injuries last year."

Collins asked, "Why would anyone want to harm her?"

"Well, I'm really not sure." He was somewhat reluctant to share his suspicions with Collins since he thought the detective might think he was jumping to conclusions. He finally continued, "The only thing that comes to mind is that she's uncovered something at her place of business that may involve considerable fraud."

Collins stared at Jack before replying and said, "How is it, Kendrick, that you get involved in all these incidents? The drug and terrorist killings a couple of years ago, the house break-in this year, and now this. Trouble just seems to follow you around, or else you're imagining things."

He paused for a moment and continued, "What kind of business is this woman involved in?"

Jack thought about replying to Collins's ridiculous comments about him personally, but he decided nothing could be gained by confronting him. As a matter of fact, he knew it stretched the imagination that one person could have been involved in so many strange incidents where he had to deal with the police in such a short period of time. He swallowed hard and said, "She works as an actuary for an insurance company, and last year during the course of her work she apparently found some irregularities and there may be fraud involved. She thinks someone is stealing from the company. She's still working on the study."

"And you really think that's enough for someone to try to murder her?"

"Look, Detective, I really don't know, and as a matter of fact, I may be dead wrong that it's connected to her job. All I know is that she's been involved in two strange accidents—either one of them could have been fatal—and the fact that a photo of her showed up at the scene on Madaket Road really makes me suspicious." Jack was getting frustrated that Collins didn't appear to be taking his concerns seriously, and with more than a little edge in his voice, he asked, "Well, what do you think?"

Collins caught the tone in Jack's question and stared at him before replying. "I need a lot more information before I can form any opinion whatsoever. I've been around here for a long time, and I've learned you don't jump at the first hint of a problem, especially when emotions are running high."

Jack held back an angry response, knowing from his experience with Collins that it would only tend to turn him off.

After several moments of silence, Collins said, "I'll run this photo through for fingerprints and then be in touch with you. I'd like to fingerprint you and the woman who was injured so that we can eliminate both of your prints from the photo."

"OK, I'll arrange with Allison to come down later today."

J ack drove back to the house, again upset with this latest experience with Collins. *How did this guy get to where he is? Even though he
has a lousy and defensive attitude in dealing with the public, you'd think that he'd
welcome any information to help in an investigation. It's sort of like he doesn't
want to complicate his life and hopes the problem will go away.*

Allison was anxious to hear what the police had to say about
the photo and actually met Jack at the door. "Well, what did they
say?"

"They're going to run the photo through to check on fingerprints, and they need both of us to go down to the station today
so they can take our prints. They want to be able to identify anyone
who's touched the photo. But the detective seemed doubtful they

would be able to find any good prints because the photo had been out in the weather for a couple of days. I don't know. We'll just have to wait and see."

"Oh, well what else did he say?"

"Look, this guy's not terribly cooperative. I've dealt with him before, and he's the kind of person who doesn't like anyone else questioning him or making suggestions."

Jack decided he had to go further with her as far as his own suspicions, but he didn't want to frighten her. "Look, Allison, I think the photo we found should make us consider some other things. You've had two accidents in less than a year, and either one of them could have been fatal."

"Yeah, I know that better than anyone."

"I don't want to be an alarmist, but when you look at the two accidents, along with your photo being found at the last one, it makes me think that we ought to consider whether they may be connected."

"Jack, what do you mean?"

Jack hesitated for a moment and then decided he had to go ahead. "Well, I'm trying not to be too suspicious, but I think we should talk about whether the accidents were deliberately aimed at injuring you personally."

Allison stared at Jack for a long time before replying. "I've been thinking about that photo all morning, and although I haven't really wanted to connect the two, I've begun to wonder the same thing. But, Jack, why would anyone want to harm me?"

Jack decided not to leap right into his theory and cautiously inquired, "Is there anything at all you can think of that would cause someone to really want to hurt you?" He added with a little humor, "Any jilted lover?"

"Look, Jack, you know me. I haven't had a relationship with anyone for so long that it's ancient history."

"I was just kidding. But, Allison, there is one thing that I do wonder about."

"What's that?" Allison replied cautiously and curiously.

"Well, the only thing that comes to my mind is this claim investigation you're involved with. If you're right and there is fraud involved, and then if the person who's behind it knows you're investigating the problem, then they may want to try to stop you."

Allison quickly replied, "Jack, I can't believe that."

"I'm trying hard not to be an alarmist, and I know my hobby of reading mysteries might make me suspicious of things that may not be there, but I think it's something we have to consider. You know you've said there's several hundred thousand dollars involved. That's enough to make some people do some crazy things."

Allison, clearly upset, stared off into the distance. After several seconds of considering the implications of what Jack was talking about, she said in a muffled voice, "I don't really want to think about this."

"I can understand. It's really frightening."

"Did you mention this to the police?"

"Yes, and I have to say that the detective thought I was jumping at things a little too quickly."

"What are they going to do?"

"Well, at this point the only thing they're doing is checking the photo for prints. I don't know where they'll go from there. I guess it depends on what they find."

Allison took a deep breath and asked, "What do you think I should do?"

Looking at Allison intently, Jack said, "I think we should consider some possibilities. When we discussed the claim study you seemed to think the person behind it was probably someone at the company."

"Yeah, I still believe that whoever pulled this off had to be very familiar with our procedures in order to work all the loopholes."

"Have you given any thought as to who it might be?"

"No, only that it has to be someone who really knows how things are done. I suppose there are a lot of possibilities. It could be someone in underwriting or claims or some experienced clerical person in administration. There are dozens of possibilities, maybe hundreds."

"Allison, it also has to be someone who's close enough to know you're conducting an investigation. How many people at the company are aware of what you've been doing and what you've found?"

"I don't really know. I expect several people in the actuarial department know that I'm working on it. You know, we talk with each other about our studies, and I've probably told at least half a dozen friends about what I've found. There're probably several others that I've casually mentioned it to over lunch or coffee, and I suppose it's possible that some of them may have mentioned it to others."

Jack thought for a minute before replying. "You mentioned to me the last time we talked that your boss wasn't really enthusiastic about your continuing the study."

"Yeah, that's right. His name is Bill Alberti. He hasn't told me to stop, but I sure get the feeling that he thinks there are more important things to do. I'm not sure why he's been so reluctant, especially since I think it may involve almost half a million dollars lost in the past five years."

Again, Jack thinking about how to proceed without going overboard. "I'm not suggesting that this guy Alberti may be the one involved in the fraud scheme, but I think you have to consider everyone, especially anyone whose behavior may be a little strange."

"Jack, I really think you're stretching now. Alberti isn't the type, and he's making plenty of money without having to commit fraud."

"OK, OK. But I think if it were me, I'd want to begin to look at all the possibilities. Incidentally, I know you're continuing to work on the study. Have you found anything more since we last talked?"

"Mainly just continued confirmation of what I found before. The disabilities are all supposed accidents, the indemnity amounts are all about the same size, the claims are all less than two months, and the policies all lapse shortly after the claim is paid. I did find out a few interesting things in the past couple of weeks. The address on all of these policies is the same, and it's a private postal box number. You know, one of those PMBs. Also, I found out the other day that all of the financial transactions, the premium payments and the claim payments, have all been done electronically. And they're all done from the same bank and with the same account number."

"Wow. That really does tie all of these phony policies and claims to the same person. Have you told your boss about this?"

"No, not the box number or the bank account number. I only discovered them a few days ago."

Neither spoke right away, and then Jack said, "Allison, I don't think you should tell your boss. If by any chance he's somehow behind this, then you don't want to let him know you may have found something that'll lead directly to whoever is responsible."

He paused and then continued, "Look, I have some pretty good contacts in the Boston area. Let me see if I can find out any more details on either the postal box number or the bank account. There's got to be a name and address, even if the name is phony."

"Yeah, I guess that's OK. I'm really scared, Jack. If what you say is right, then they may try to hurt me again."

"I know it must be frightening, but I think we've got to do a little poking around on our own."

"Don't you think we should let the police handle it?"

"I think we need a little more information before they'll really listen to us. How about letting me check out some things over the next few days—say until next Wednesday or Thursday?"

"I hate to involve you in this, Jack. I just want this all to stop! Yeah, OK, I guess I can wait a few days."

"In the meantime, Allison, I think you should stay away from any bike riding, and I don't think it's a good idea for you to go out alone."

44

August 2009

Al Collins walked into the chief's office with more than his usual air of superiority. This was one of the most important investigations he'd ever been involved in, and he'd just broken it wide open. The chief would have to be impressed, and maybe this would really seal his chances of succeeding the chief in a couple of years when he retired.

One of the fingerprints on the photo of Allison Sheppard had matched those of a petty criminal who was well known to the police. Phil Costa had lived on the island for years and bounced around from one job to another. He had been arrested twice in the past for petty theft and had spent a couple of months in the county jail. The police record showed there was suspicion of his having a drug habit, but nothing had ever been proved.

After he was arrested, police confronted Costa with the evidence of his fingerprints on the photograph, and Costa became increasingly nervous. Under persistent interrogation, he finally admitted that he had put the wire across the bike path, but he said it was intended to be only a prank and he really didn't intend to injure anyone.

Collins's physical size loomed over the much smaller Costa, and he said, "Oh, come on, Costa, you had to know there was a good chance that someone would be injured. For Christ's sake, that wire could have killed someone."

"I just did it for a lark."

"How did you happen to have this photo of the person who was injured?"

"I've never seen it before."

"Come on, Phil, your fingerprints are all over it."

Costa remained quiet.

"You're not making sense. Why would you go out there early in the morning just for the hell of it to set up the wire? You're not leveling with me. Do you think I'm that stupid to believe this crazy story?"

Costa was clearly uncomfortable and increasingly nervous, and he simply stared at his hands, unable to think of any reasonable answer.

"Did someone put you up to this?"

Costa shook his head but didn't reply. The more the detective confronted him the more he clearly went into his shell. Collins waited for several moments and then said, "OK, I've wasted enough time listening to your fairy tales. I'm holding you here for a couple of days to let you think over what really happened. Maybe that'll help your memory. You're in serious trouble, Phil. You've seriously injured someone and could have killed her." In an attempt to frighten Costa further, he concluded, "I can charge you for attempted murder, and you'll be put away for a long time."

After two days in the cell Costa had become extremely agitated, and Collins was convinced he was indeed an addict and suffering from withdrawal. He waited until late in the afternoon that day and then brought Costa into the interrogation room. He told him he didn't believe his story and was going to keep him locked up until he got to the truth, and again he threatened to charge him with attempted murder. After a half hour of more persistent questioning, Costa began to open up. He admitted that Tony Andrews had asked him to put the wire on the path so that this woman would be thrown from her bike. He nervously still insisted there was no intent to seriously injure her, only to frighten her.

When Collins asked him why he agreed to injure someone he didn't even know, Costa said it was for money. When Collins pressed him for how much he was paid, Costa lied again and said it was around two thousand dollars.

"That's a lot of money for staging an accident just to frighten someone. Come on, Costa, what aren't you telling me?"

"I don't know. That's what I was told to do."

"Look, Costa, I know you're a druggie, and I think you used that money to get a fix. And I don't think you're telling me the whole story about why you strung out that wire. I think we'll just keep you here for another couple of days and see if your memory gets any better." After waiting a minute to gauge Costa's reaction, he then continued, "On the other hand, if you level with me, perhaps I can let you out today."

Costa was quiet, but his hands definitely showed an increasing tremor.

Collins said, "Why did Andrews want this girl injured?"

"I don't know. I didn't ask."

"You mean as long as the money was there you didn't care?"

"Yeah, I guess that's right."

"Where do you get the drugs to feed your habit?"

Costa stared at Collins for an uncomfortable period of time, saying nothing, and when the detective finally got up, he said, "You're going back to your cell!"

Two hours later Costa asked to talk with Collins again. As Collins walked into the cell, it was obvious that Costa was truly at the breaking point. Collins thought to himself, *The combination of more than two days without a fix, sitting in a cell, and the pressure of interrogation has finally brought him to the point where maybe I can find out what's really behind this.*

"I'm busy, Costa. Why did you want to see me?"

"If I give you some more information, will you let me go?"

"It'll depend upon what information you have and if you're telling me the whole truth. I'm through with your line of bullshit."

Costa paused and then, physically shaking, he said, "OK, Tony Andrews did ask me to set up the accident, and he paid me off in heroin. I've been trying to break the habit for a long time, but I just can't."

Under further interrogation, Costa admitted that Andrews had been his supplier for more than a year. When Collins asked him how he paid for all these drugs, Costa at first said he paid with cash. The detective then pressed him on where he got that amount of cash to feed his habit. Costa initially said nothing in reply, but when the detective threatened to leave him in the cell for another day, he completely broke down. He admitted that he had broken into several homes over the winter and that Andrews always took the stolen property in exchange for the drugs. He further admitted he knew of others who were also paying for drugs by stealing from the seasonal homes that were vacant. And under still further questioning, he gave Collins the names of three other local residents who he said were also trading stolen property to Andrews for drugs.

Collins was elated that this seemingly prank accident on the bike path had led him to solving the rash of break-ins. After explaining and detailing the information to the chief, he asked for authorization to arrest Tony Andrews and to get a search warrant for his property. He wanted to move quickly before Andrews had an opportunity to dispose of either the stolen goods or any drugs that might be on the property.

Later that day the police arrested Tony Andrews, and the next morning they searched his property. The police found several TVs, DVD players, VCRs, and computers that Andrews had kept in a locked storeroom, and many of the items matched the description of recently stolen property. In addition, after a careful search of Andrews's house, the police had found a supply of heroin locked in a closet. There was enough to take care of the island's drug-using population for several weeks.

Under interrogation, Andrews steadfastly refused to talk and quickly insisted on seeing his attorney. He neither confirmed nor denied Costa's allegations that he was the supplier of the drugs or that he had been the recipient of the stolen property. Collins was so elated to have solved the stolen property investigation and uncovered the source of the drug supply that he ignored entirely any questioning of Andrews concerning Allison's accident on the bike path.

And so, since Tony Andrews was not questioned as to why he had hired Costa to set up the accident, there was no reason for Andrews to have to reveal his conspiracy with Dick Gimble on the bike path.

45

August 2009

Allison became increasingly alarmed the more she thought about her conversation with Jack and his suspicions. On the one hand, she couldn't believe the two incidents that she initially thought were accidents were actually deliberate attempts to injure or, in fact, kill her. And then, the thought that the accidents were linked to her actuarial study was too much to digest. But the existence of the photo at the scene of the bike path incident just could not be explained away. *If Jack is right and someone wants to stop me from continuing the investigation, then they'll probably try again. What can I do to stop this craziness? Maybe if I abandon the study and let the word get out that I've stopped, then perhaps whoever is behind this will stop also. I just can't believe anyone at the company is involved in this. I told Jack I'd wait a few days before going to the police, but I can't sit here and do nothing.*

She picked up the phone that evening and called Dick Gimble.

"Hi, Dick, this is Allison. Do you have few minutes to talk?"

He was startled to hear her voice. "Oh hi, Allison. What's up?"

"Well, it's a long and crazy story, but two days ago I had another bike accident."

Feigning surprise, Dick replied, "You've got to be kidding. Were you injured?"

"No, not badly, just some cuts and bruises. But that's not the main thing. There's reason to believe the accident may be connected to my claim investigation."

Dick literally jumped up from his chair and began to pace the room while still holding the phone. "What are you talking about?"

Allison took a deep breath before continuing and replied, "It's crazy, but they found a photograph of me at the scene. It was a small, pocket-sized photo, and I think it's a copy of the one the company keeps in my personnel file."

Dick, trying to appear ignorant said, "How could that have gotten there?"

"I don't know."

"Are you sure it didn't fall out of your wallet or clothing?"

Allison, a little irritated, said, "No, Dick, why would I carry around a picture of myself?"

"I don't know. It just seems so weird."

"Well, don't you see? It looks like the person who strung the wire across the bike path had a picture so he could identify me, and he must have dropped it by accident."

Dick, trying to clear his mind, decided he needed to find out more about what Allison had done with the picture. "Where's the picture now?"

"The police have it, and they're running some fingerprint tests."

Pacing more rapidly and with perspiration standing out on his forehead, Dick quickly thought to himself, *Can they trace any prints on the photo back to me? That goddamn idiot friend of Tony's. His prints are probably all over it.*

Allison continued, "They apparently don't think they're going to find anything usable because the photo had been on the ground overnight, and I guess it was damp or something." And then she continued, "Amy's husband thinks that my boss may have something to do with it."

"Why would he think that?"

"Well, he's been dragging his feet about my continuing the study, and Jack thinks that may be because he doesn't want to be found out. There's a large amount of money involved."

"Wow, that's unbelievable." Quickly thinking that maybe this would steer her away from any suspicions toward him, Dick asked, "What do you think?"

"I don't know what to think. I can't see Bill either stealing from the company or physically trying to hurt someone. But I can't think of anyone else."

"What are you going to do next?"

"Well, that's really why I called you. There are a couple of things I've learned that you may be able to help me with."

Dick replied, "What's that?"

"Do you remember when I last talked with you I mentioned that all of the claims were using the same private mailbox?"

Dick hesitated and thought, *Where the hell is she going with this?* He replied, "Yeah, I think I remember you saying it was somewhere in the Natick area."

"Well, since then I've found out from the company records that all of the financial transactions are done electronically, both the premium payments and the claim payments, and they all use the same bank account number."

Dick was too shaken to reply, and Allison continued, "Well, I wonder if there's any way you can check to find out who this box number really belongs to, or whose name is on the bank account? The person behind this must have filled out some kind of an application for either the postal box or the bank account, or for both."

"Offhand, I don't know just how I'd go about it, but let me give it some thought. Have you told anyone else about this?"

"No, I haven't dared to tell anyone at the company. The only other person who knows is Amy's husband. I haven't mentioned it to the police yet, and in fact, they haven't seemed particularly interested in anything to do with this."

"Well, I think it's a good idea to wait until you have more information before you take it any further." Trying hard to stay focused and appear cooperative, he continued, "Why don't you give me the details on the box number and the bank account, and I'll see what I can find out."

Allison gave Dick the information, and he told her he'd try to get back to her in a couple of days.

46

The stress on Dick Gimble was clearly showing. He couldn't remember the last time he had a restful night's sleep, he had developed visible dark rings under his eyes, and during the day at work he was nervous and jumpy. His friends recognized the change in his demeanor, but when they asked him if anything was wrong, his temper quickly flared. He was getting close to the emotional breaking point.

The night following the latest telephone conversation with Allison was perhaps the worst he had experienced. The day at work had dragged on, and he found his mind continually drifting away from his claim work, unable to concentrate for more than a few minutes. Over and over in his mind he kept running over the same thoughts. *I have to do something. I can't let this thing go on. It's about ready to blow up in my face, and I can't let that happen. What the hell am I going to do? I can't let her dig into the details of the study any further. I've got to do something now.*

Ed Fletcher called Dick close to the end of the work day. "Dick, I need to see you. Can we get together after work?"

Not wanting to talk with Ed or anyone, he said, "I've got some plans this evening. What's up anyway?"

Ed hesitated for only a moment and said, "Look, I only need a few minutes. Can you meet me out in the parking lot after work?"

Dick had begun to formulate a plan for dealing with Allison and said, "I can only spare a few minutes, and I'm leaving right at five o'clock."

"OK, I'll be in the lot a couple of minutes after five."

When Ed got out to his car, Dick was already waiting. He unlocked the doors, and they both climbed into the front seat. Dick said, "OK, what's goin' on?"

Ed looked out the front windshield, and avoiding direct eye contact with Dick, he replied, "Dick, I can't go on like this any longer. I'm a physical wreck worrying about when this investigation is going to lead to us, and I don't see how we can avoid it." He hesitated for several moments, made a loud sigh, and continued, "I think we should go to the company and tell them about what we did."

"What the hell are you talking about? You're absolutely crazy. For Christ's sake, that's the dumbest thing I've ever heard. Are you ready to go to jail?"

Ed finally turned to Dick and, almost pleading, said, "Look, hear me out! I think at some point this actuary's investigation is going to lead to us. She's like a goddamn pit bull and isn't going to let up. You know, both the mailbox number and the bank account can be traced to me if someone is persistent."

"Christ, I know all about that. Maybe you're ready to go to prison, but I'm not."

Ed continued, "I think if we went to the company in the right way, with the right story, they might not go to the police. But if we wait until this finally blows up in our faces, then we're dealing with the police."

"You don't think the company will go to the cops if we go to them first?"

"I think it depends on how we go about it. Supposing we went to them and said we started this thing out as a lark, a prank, and it simply got out of hand. We were initially just trying to show how lax some of the company procedures were. We could offer to pay back the money."

"Jesus Christ, Ed, you're dreaming. You're in fantasyland. They'll turn us over to the cops before you even finish your crazy story."

Ed returned to staring out the window and persistently said, "I don't know about that. The company doesn't want bad publicity, especially in this town where it goes out of its way to protect its reputation. An insurance company wants to appear sound and secure to the public, and bad publicity does just the opposite. I think they might want to handle it themselves and not go to the police."

"Ed, it just doesn't fly."

"Dick, I've thought a lot about this, and I don't agree. I think there's a good chance of this keeping us out of jail. I know we'll lose our jobs, but that's better than the alternative." He paused one more time and continued, "I've decided I'm going to go ahead."

Dick turned to Ed, grabbed his shirt, and pulled him toward him so their faces were almost touching. His face had become reddened, and he shouted at Ed, "Look, you stupid asshole, that's not going to happen. You'll end up in the clink the next day." He stopped for only a moment, but realizing that he had to do something to keep Ed from going to the company, he said, "If you go to the company, you're going to be charged with more than fraud or stealing—whatever the hell they'll call it."

"What're you talking about?"

Still grasping Ed's shirt and staring straight into his eyes, he said, "Allison Sheppard's bike accident a year ago was no accident."

"What do you mean?"

"I was the one who forced her off the road down in Upton."

Ed pulled away from Dick's grasp and said, "You did what?"

"I thought that if she was really seriously injured or killed, then the study would stop. I didn't see any other way."

Ed was almost speechless, but he muttered, "You crazy bastard."

Dick, still unsure of what Ed would do and knowing he had to shock him into keeping quiet, said, "That's not all. She had a second accident a few days ago, and she's now suspicious that the two are linked and may be tied to the claim study."

Ed was silent, finally realizing how serious the situation had become.

Dick needed to frighten Ed even further into not going to the company, so he said, "You're as involved in this as I am, and there's no way this'll be kept away from the police if you go to the company. We're talking about assault and maybe even attempted murder. The only way to keep this from happening is to make absolutely certain the study is stopped—stopped now."

Ed, barely speaking above a whisper, "And how are you going to do that?"

"I'm on my way to Nantucket tonight, and I'm going to put an end to this study once and for all."

Ed was staring at him, trying to comprehend what he was hearing. As Dick opened the door to leave the car, he said to Ed, "Don't do anything stupid that'll get us both put away for the rest of our lives. I'll call you tomorrow."

47

August 2009—Wednesday

Since his return to Boston following Allison's accident on the bike path, Jack Kendrick had been busy in every spare moment thinking about how he would go about finding out who was behind the claim fraud scheme. He continued to be convinced that if he could identify that person, then he'd also have found who was responsible for the two accidents. It still seemed to him that Allison's boss was the most likely suspect, even though she was convinced otherwise.

Although Jack wished the Nantucket police had taken him more seriously, he was secretly excited about pursuing the unanswered questions on his own. His fascination with mysteries drove this excitement, and his thinking naturally and sometimes uncontrollably imagined all sorts of conspiracies. In this mind-set, he was convinced that someone had tried twice to seriously injure or even kill Allison, and he also was certain they would try again.

On Monday morning he had gone to his local bank in Quincy in hopes of their being able to tell him what bank belonged to the bank code that Allison had obtained from the company records. He knew that banks were very protective of customer privacy, and so he had concocted a story he hoped would get him the desired information. He told them he had received a check in his photography business that had been returned by the bank because of insufficient funds. He needed to find the person who wrote the check and thought the best way was to work through the bank on which the check had been written. His acquaintance at his own bank did not hesitate to tell him that the bank involved was in Natick, but he said that he doubted whether they would give out any detailed information about their depositors.

Jack left work early that day and drove out to Natick. He changed his story a little when he met one of the bank officers, explaining that a customer had given him a check for a framed photograph but had failed to sign the check. He gave the officer the personal account number that Allison had found in the company system, and he told him he needed his help to locate the person since there was no address on the check. The officer turned to his computer and quickly pulled up a record and said, "Yes, that's an active account with us, but I can't give you any personal information without the customer's authorization. I can tell you that the name on the account is that of a business, not an individual, and that the only address I have is a postal box number. If you like, I'll call the business and ask for permission to give out the information."

Jack hesitated and thought to himself, *Chances are the name on the account is a phony business. I don't want to tip off whoever is behind this that someone is trying to find them.* He thought of one more possibility and asked, "Can you tell me if the postal box is a regular U.S. postal box, or is it the address to one of those private boxes? I think they're called PMBs."

The officer looked at the computer screen and then at Jack. "Well, I don't see how this will help you, but it is a private postal box."

"Well, thanks for your time anyway."

As Jack left, he thought, *Well, that wasn't a lot of help. But at least I've confirmed that the postal box is not a U.S. post office box, and it sounds like the same type that was used in the fraud scheme. But I still have to find out who's behind it.*

He then drove to the address of the postal box firm that he had received from Allison, hoping to get more information. He adjusted his story again and told the clerk he had received a letter where the return address was a postal box at this address, but he needed to get hold of the person and didn't have the street address.

The clerk said, "I'm not permitted to give out any personal information."

Jack at this point wasn't ready to give up quietly and asked, "Can you give me the box holder's telephone number?"

The clerk thought for a moment and said, "Yeah, I don't see any harm in that." And he gave the number to Jack.

As Jack left, he pondered how he could get the address now that he had the telephone number. He recalled that someone had told him if you went on the Internet you could do a search and find either telephone numbers or addresses by entering one or the other. It was too late to pursue the puzzle further that evening, but when he got back home, he immediately went to the computer and typed into Google "telephone numbers." A screen popped up and gave him a menu of choices. He scanned over the choices and found one that said "reverse numbers." He typed in the telephone number, and immediately the screen showed the following:

Edwin G. Fletcher
Garden Apartments, Apt. 309
938 Boston Turnpike Road
Natick, MA

He wrote down the information and then typed in the telephone number again to make certain he had not made an error. The same name appeared again. He then wondered if the Internet would have any information on this individual. He typed in "Edwin G. Fletcher" and waited a few moments, and the screen finally showed a list of several people with the last name of Fletcher. He quickly found the name he was looking for that listed the same address he had just found. He clicked on that name, and the screen revealed that this person was an insurance underwriter who worked for the John Adams Insurance Company.

Jack said, "Bingo! I've found the bastard."

48

Thursday

Jack went to his photo shop in Quincy Market very early in the morning. He had slept fitfully and woken up thinking about what his next step would be. He wasn't ready to go back to the police until he had some more definite information. *This guy Fletcher hasn't come up in any of my conversations with Allison, and I still wonder if her boss, Bill Alberti, is in some way involved in the scheme. Perhaps the two were somehow working the fraud together.*

He spent every spare minute during the day thinking about how he would proceed. He decided to call Allison that evening, but with some reluctance because he didn't want to alarm her any more than she was already.

"Allison, do you know anyone at your company named Edwin Fletcher?"

Allison replied, "No, I don't think so. The name Fletcher sounds a little familiar, but we have close to two thousand people at the company. I sure don't know them all. Why do you ask?"

"Well, I'm still trying to chase down the information you gave me—the bank account and the post office box number. This guy Fletcher's name came up, but I'm not sure it means anything and thought you might be able to help. He's an underwriter at your company."

"Sorry I can't help." She paused and then continued, "Jack, I think we should take the information and go to the police."

"Give me another day, Allison."

49

Friday

Jack drove out to Natick again late on Friday afternoon. He grabbed a quick bite to eat at a McDonald's and put together in his mind how he would approach Fletcher. He was a little apprehensive that, when he confronted him, Fletcher might become violent. *This guy has tried to kill Allison twice. I'll have to proceed carefully.* When he arrived at the apartment building on busy Route 9, also called the Boston Turnpike, he found a five-story brick building that must have had close to one hundred units.

He waited outside until around six thirty, hoping this would have left enough time for Fletcher to have arrived home from work. He was prepared to wait until late in the evening if he wasn't there. In the entryway of the building, he found Fletcher's name on the intercom system. He punched in the apartment number 309 and waited for someone to answer. He was about to hang up the phone when Fletcher answered.

"Yes."

Jack quickly said, "Mr. Fletcher, my name is Jack Ashton, and I work for WBOS-TV in Boston. I'm on special assignment and wonder if you could spare a few minutes?"

"What's this all about?"

"Well, I'm preparing a report on insurance company underwriting practices, and I know you work for John Adams Insurance. I've been told that you're an experienced underwriter, and I have some questions I hope you can help me with."

"What kind of a report, and how did you get my name?"

"We've been talking with several employees of many different companies, and your name was given to me by someone at your company." Jack had to find the right words to get Fletcher to let him in. "The report is about what practices insurance companies use in qualifying individuals for coverage."

"Look, I don't know if I can help you out. Are you sure the company knows you're doing this survey?"

Jack was getting anxious and fearful that he'd come away with nothing. "Your company is aware I've been talking to a lot of employees, but of course you're free to fill them in on our conversation. This'll only take a few minutes."

Fletcher gripped the phone nervously and said, "OK, but I have to go out in about fifteen minutes." He pressed the buzzer to allow Jack to enter the building.

Jack immediately sized up the man and was relieved to see Fletcher was physically much smaller than he was, and his somewhat limp and clammy handshake sort of reassured him that Fletcher didn't appear to be the aggressive type. He briefly showed Fletcher his press pass that he still carried from his days when he worked for WBOS.

Jack launched right into his questions. He decided to confront Fletcher directly and get right into his real reason for being there. "Thank you for agreeing to see me. I should tell you up front that this report also deals with some claim irregularities."

Fletcher was taken aback and quickly said, "I don't work in the claim department."

"Yes, I know that, but your name has come up while we've been investigating the possibility of claim fraud at your company. I thought you could help us clear up some questions."

Fletcher was almost speechless. He became noticeably uneasy and stammered, "I don't know what you're talking about."

"Well, we've found the same post office box number listed as the address on dozens of disability insurance applications at John Adams over the past few years. We think these applications are phony, and we know that someone has been submitting dozens of fraudulent claims."

Fletcher's face had become reddened, and perspiration began to appear on his forehead. "I really don't know what you're talking about."

Jack clearly recognized that he had upset Fletcher and wanted to press the advantage before he could regain his composure. "I wanted to give you an opportunity to explain how come your box number is the one listed as the address of record on all these policies. It's the address where all of the correspondence for these policies was sent."

Fletcher looked at Jack and realized that he couldn't continue to play entirely ignorant. He had to admit to something. "Look, this whole thing was really a lark. We were trying to find a way to point out to the company that some of its practices had big loopholes." And then after a pause he added, "It sort of got out of hand."

Jack said, "Out of hand to the tune of tens of thousands, perhaps hundreds of thousands of dollars?"

Fletcher, now talking very rapidly with a tremor in his voice, said, "You may not believe this, but I had planned to go to the company next week and explain this whole thing. I intend to pay back all the money."

Jack tried to look him squarely in the eye, but Fletcher avoided his gaze. Jack said very sternly, "Mr. Fletcher, there's more to this than just money."

"What are you talking about?"

"Does the name Allison Sheppard mean anything to you?"

Fletcher stood up and shouted at Jack, "Look, I had nothing to do with that. I didn't even know about the accident until he mentioned it to me today."

"Who is he? Are you talking about Bill Alberti?"

"No, no, not Alberti, I'm talking about Dick."

Fletcher had now gone so far with the story that he had no choice but to continue. "Dick Gimble. He's a claim examiner, and this whole thing was his idea. I tried to get him to stop it right after we first started, but he had some serious money problems and wouldn't stop."

Jack was about to reply when he suddenly stopped and his face took on an anguished and startled look. It had taken him a second to remember Dick Gimble as the friend of Allison's who had come to Nantucket.

"Where does Gimble live?"

"He lives in another apartment block, farther down Route 9, but he's not there tonight."

"Where can I find him?"

Fletcher lowered his head and said in a low voice, "He told me this afternoon he was on his way to Nantucket."

"You mean he was going there tonight?"

"Yes." And then, lying to avoid admitting he knew something about Gimble's immediate plans, he said, "I don't know really why he went. He's had a few dates with Allison during the past few months. I guess he went down there to see her."

Jack, fearful of the implications of what he had just heard, said, "Mr. Fletcher, you're in real big trouble. I'd suggest you go to your company management and the police right away. You'll be in a lot bigger trouble if something should happen to Allison Sheppard in the meantime."

Visibly shaken himself, Jack quickly left the apartment without a further word.

Friday Evening

Dick Gimble's mind was in overdrive. He was focused on one thing, and that was to stop Allison Sheppard from pursuing her investigation any further. His anger and frustration had clouded all reason from his thinking, and he was not even considering the ramifications of his actions if he should be caught.

The drive to Hyannis was normally a little more than an hour; however, as he drove down Route 3, it began to rain, and along with the increased Friday evening traffic, everything began to slow down considerably. When he reached Hyannis, he stopped at a gas station and purchased a two-gallon gas can. He took his workout clothes out of the gym bag in the trunk and placed the empty can in it.

He got to the airport, went to the ACK Airlines counter, paid cash for a ticket on the small nine-passenger 402 Cessna to Nantucket, and checked the gym bag. Security on this flight was minimal, and he had no difficulty in giving an alias for his name, and the only personal information they requested was how much he weighed. This airline always requested the weight of all passengers in order to distribute the weight properly in the small aircraft, and it was humorous to observe some passengers whispering their weight to the clerk so that others could not hear.

The flight was supposed to leave at seven thirty, but because of the rain it was delayed about fifteen minutes. Dick could not sit down in the waiting area, but kept pacing, anxious to get on with his task. The normally short twenty-minute flight to its island destination took more than thirty minutes because of the weather, and Dick, for the first time, began to worry about what things could go wrong with his plan. *What if Allison isn't there? What if I'm seen before I get the job done? What if I'm caught before I get off the island?* His momentary fears were overtaken by the need to make certain that the claim investigation was terminated.

After the plane landed, he went to the local rent-a-car desk, used a fake ID he still carried around from his college days, and paid cash for the rental. He stopped at the gas station just outside of the airport and filled the can up with gas.

He then drove the four miles to the street where Amy and Jack's house was located and slowly drove by the house. It was now after eight thirty, and because of the dark cloud cover, the house lights were on even though it was early August. He noticed the car in the garage and also a light in the room over the garage, the room that he knew was the one where Allison slept. He heaved a sigh of relief that at least one of his concerns about the plan working appeared to be eliminated.

He drove by the house again, taking in all of the surroundings to make certain he had not neglected any detail in his plan. He thought to himself, *Everything seems to be set. Now all I have to do is wait for them to go to bed.* He remembered that because of the young children the family tended to go to bed early, and he knew that Allison did also since she regularly got up before six o'clock every morning to go through her daily exercise routine. When he once again drove by, it was a little after nine thirty, and he noticed that all of the lights were finally off.

51

Friday Evening—7:00 p.m.

Jack Kendrick had left Fletcher's apartment hurriedly and was indeed fearful of what he had learned. *It looks like this bastard, Gimble, is behind the whole scheme, and if that's the case, then he's undoubtedly somehow involved in Allison's accidents. I've got to warn her that he's on his way to Nantucket and that she may be in danger again. Jesus Christ, Amy and the kids may be in danger also.*

When he got to his car, he called the Nantucket house, but there was no answer. He left an urgent message for Amy or Allison to call him on his cell phone as soon as they got the message.

He then called the Nantucket Police Department. "I'd like to speak with Detective Collins."

"He's not on duty right now. Can I help you?"

"I'm calling from off island. This is an emergency, and I need to speak with someone who can stop a crime before it happens. I have reason to believe that someone may be on their way to the island to murder someone who's at my home."

"What is your name, please?"

Jack was frustrated that he had to take time to give out personal information, but he knew this was normal police procedure. "My name is Jack Kendrick, k-e-n-d-r-i-c-k, and I have a summer home on 15 Patriot Lane. My wife and family are at this address now."

"Mr. Kendrick, I'm going to transfer you to Officer Hines."

Officer Hines came on the phone and asked Jack what the problem was, and Jack repeated the same information he had given previously. Jack recalled Hines was the one who had come to his house when it had been burglarized during the previous winter. He reminded Hines of who he was, and Hines acknowledged that he remembered the incident.

Hines asked, "Can you give me some details as to why you think your family is in danger and that someone's about to commit a crime?"

Jack tried with great difficulty to keep his composure and to make his explanation concise. He explained his previous discussion with Detective Collins about the accident on the bike path, and that he was certain that someone was trying to harm or kill Allison. He told Hines about the claim study and that he was certain it was linked to the accidents. He then went on to describe his meeting with Ed Fletcher and that he had been told that Gimble was on his way to Nantucket that evening. He said he didn't know the reason for Gimble going to the island, but he felt that he would likely make another attempt on Allison's life.

Hines asked Jack questions as to how and when Gimble was getting to the island, and Jack said he didn't know, but of course, it had to be by either ferry or plane.

Hines then said, "Incidentally, I'm aware of the incident on the bike path. We've identified the culprit through fingerprints, and he's been arrested, but I don't think that incident is at all connected with this claim investigation you're talking about."

Jack replied, "How do you know it's not connected?"

"Well, there's no way for me to be sure, but this guy was a druggie and has led us to breaking up a large drug ring on the island. As a matter of fact, we've found that the drug ring was tied to all of the break-ins, like yours, last winter. A whole group of drug addicts were breaking into summer homes, stealing electronic equipment, and then swapping the stolen goods for heroin. The dealer was a guy who runs a secondhand store on the island. We think his only motive was a robbery, but someone stopped to help before he was able to get to the biker who was injured."

Jack sat up, alert, and asked, "Was the secondhand dealer a guy by the name of Andrews?"

"Yeah, and your stolen goods undoubtedly went through him also."

Jack, remembering the mantel clock that was in the store and his conversation with Detective Collins, said, "I had a conversation with Collins a few weeks ago about my suspicions of this guy Andrews."

Hines said, "Look, there's nothing to link Gimble to the bike path incident. There may be some reasonable explanation for why he's coming to the island, but I'll take a run by the house right now and continue to have our patrols go by regularly throughout the evening and the night."

"OK, and thanks, but you have to know I believe this guy may be dangerous."

"Yeah, I understand your concern, and I assure you we'll take the necessary precautions. Can you describe this guy Gimble?"

Jack did his best to recall and describe what Gimble looked like based on the one brief time he had met him. As Hines hung up,

Jack thought to himself, *Well, at least I'm sure glad I got Hines on the phone rather than Collins.*

Jack had no sooner hung up than he remembered Allison had said that this guy Gimble, when he visited her, was staying with a secondhand dealer on the island. At the time Jack didn't pay any attention to it, but now he was certain that the secondhand dealer must have been Andrews. *Jesus Christ, that's another link that ties Gimble to Allison's accidents. There are just too many coincidences leading to him. Fletcher said he's the one behind the claim fraud scheme, and he was on Nantucket just before the bike path accident. The photo I found at the accident was from the John Adams Insurance Company files where he probably could have gotten it, and he's apparently a friend of this guy Andrews, who is linked to the guy they say caused the bike path accident. Probably this guy was paid off in drugs to put the wire on the path. And now Gimble is on his way to Nantucket.*

He thought about calling back Officer Hines to let him know Gimble's connection with the secondhand store, but he concluded that the police were doing everything they could at this time. He tried again to call Amy at home, but there was still no answer. Even though he preferred to talk with her in person, the situation was potentially so dangerous that he left another voice message: "Amy or Allison, whoever gets this message first, during my investigation of the post office box numbers Allison gave me I've found that they lead to Dick Gimble, the guy who came to the island to visit Allison. There's no question in my mind he's the one behind the fraud scheme, and I think he's also behind Allison's accidents. I know this may sound crazy and will be a shock to Allison, but tell her that I'm sure. I learned a few minutes ago he's on his way to the island this evening, and I think he may be planning another attempt to hurt Allison or worse. I want all of you to get out of the house tonight. Find somewhere to go. I've called the Nantucket police, and they said they'll check on the house, but I think you should all get out immediately. I'm on my way to Hyannis and will try to get the late plane. Please call me on my cell phone as soon as you get this and let me know where you've gone."

He closed the phone and concentrated on his driving. The rain had gotten worse in the past hour, and he was certain that the last plane was at eight thirty. He would either just make it or just miss it, and he leaned on the accelerator pedal more as he saw the speedometer creep past seventy-five and then eighty. It was a risky speed in these weather conditions, but the traffic on the highway had eased and he really had no choice.

Throughout the ride he could not get his mind off the threat to his family. He was naturally concerned for Allison, but his wife and children were foremost in his mind. He tried to call Amy again, but there was still no answer. He tried her cell phone, but the recorded voice message clearly indicated that it wasn't turned on.

He arrived at the small airport a few minutes before eight thirty. Rather than leave his car in the parking lot, which was some distance from the terminal, he pulled up in front of the terminal into the fifteen-minute parking spaces. He knew he would be ticketed or towed, but that was furthest from his concerns. He ran through the rain into the terminal and up to the ACK Airlines counter.

"Can you get me on the eight thirty flight to Nantucket?"

"Well, we've got space, but right now nothing's moving. The airport's down in Nantucket because of the heavy rain and poor visibility."

"Do you expect it will open up later?"

"I can't say. It's been bad all evening, but so far every flight has eventually gotten off. Since this is the last flight, we'll wait for at least a half hour before canceling it."

Thinking about an alternative way to get to the island, Jack asked, "Do you know when the last ferry is?"

"I'm afraid it left a few minutes ago. We had a lot of our passengers choose to go that way."

Jack finally said, "Well, book me on this flight. I have an emergency and don't have any choice."

He found a chair and immediately pulled out his cell phone and called Amy again, and still there was no answer at either the house or on her cell phone.

He called the Nantucket police again and asked for Officer Hines, but he was told Hines was out on patrol and that no one else could give him any information about his situation. They promised to have Hines call him when he returned.

52

Saturday—1:00 a.m.

Gimble continued to drive by the house every hour to make certain there were no lights and no activity of any kind. Twice he had seen a police car in the area and assumed it was some normal patrol going by the house about every half hour. *I'll have to be careful about that since I can't be certain the patrol is really on a fixed schedule.* At about one o'clock in the morning, he was certain that everyone was into a deep sleep. He parked the car on a small dirt road some seventy-five yards from the house, took the can of gas, and walked quickly down the dark, unlit street, being especially alert to any cars that might turn onto this little-used road. He observed the house again; the car was still in the garage, and that reassured him they were all in the house.

He knew the dark, rainy evening was a real advantage; however, he was getting wet in spite of the fact the rain had begun to let up. His eyesight became used to the dark, and as he quietly approached the garage, he took out a small penlight from his pocket. He didn't want to trip over something in the garage.

He took the cover off the can and first began pouring and splashing the gasoline under the car. His idea had been to make it look as if the fire was started by some malfunction in the car's hot engine. He made certain the area under the engine was soaked with the fuel in hopes it would then ignite the oil around the engine block, increase the intensity of the fire, and be consistent with the engine being the source. He needed to make the incident truly look like an accident.

He splashed the remaining gas in the can on the interior walls of the garage and over the workbench where there were some cans of paint. He needed to make sure the fire spread rapidly to the room over the garage where Allison lay sleeping.

Finally he pulled from his pocket a book of matches. The fumes from the spilled gasoline were truly getting intense by this time, and he moved outside the garage away from where he expected the fumes to ignite. He bent to shield the matches from the rain, lit one, and then lit the entire book. He moved toward the garage door and quickly threw the burning book into the garage.

There was an immediate and loud whoosh, and the flames and intense heat caught Gimble by surprise. He jumped back quickly, but even with his prepared caution the heat was intense enough he thought his clothes might be on fire and that his face had been burned. As he ran away down the driveway, he realized he had only felt the initial heat from the fuel being ignited and that he had escaped any injury or damage.

He ran quickly to his rented car, put the empty gas can in the trunk, and drove out of the dirt road toward the house. The entire process had taken no more than ten minutes. As he approached the building, he could see the fire reflected above the house even in the rain, and as he drew abreast of the house, he saw that the garage was fully engulfed in flames. Smoke was pouring out of the room above the garage. There were no lights on anywhere in the house. He thought briefly of the other people sleeping in the main part of the building, but at this point his mind was so disturbed that he didn't really care whether others were killed or not. *It would serve this guy Kendrick right for meddling in something that was none of his business.*

The house was far enough away from neighboring homes that he was confident the fire would have done its job before it was discovered. He continued to be alert for the police patrol car, but as he turned from Patriot Lane onto the Madaket Road, there was no sign of it.

On the main road he picked up his speed and drove back toward the airport. Several minutes later he passed the fire department on Sparks Avenue and was relieved to see there was no activity there. He was now secure in the belief that enough time had elapsed for the fire to have done its work. He drove down Old South Road to the airport.

He hadn't made plans as to where he would sleep, but it was certainly too risky to rent a room for the night, so he decided to sleep in the rented car. It was after one thirty in the morning when he reached the parking area for rental cars at the airport. There was no security in the small rent-a-car lot, so he pulled the car into a spot away from any lights, turned off the engine, pushed the seat back into a reclining position, leaned back, and tried to relax.

53

Saturday—3:00 a.m.

Jack was having a fitful sleep, angry and frustrated that the flight had been finally canceled at nine thirty last evening and there was no other way to get to the island. He was most especially worried that he had not been able to get hold of Amy to make certain she had either received his message or that the police had told her to leave the house. He had left the airport, gotten into his car, and checked in at the Marriott Courtyard, a short distance from the airport. He left another message for Amy on her cell phone and told her he planned to catch an early flight to Nantucket first thing in the morning.

As he tried again to doze off, his cell phone rang. He quickly came alert and said, "Amy, is that you?"

Jack was startled to hear Officer Hines's voice say, "No, Mr. Kendrick, this is Officer Hines from the Nantucket Police Department. I'm sorry to bother you at this hour, but I knew you'd want to know that there's been an incident at your house."

Jack sat up in bed and urgently asked, "What do you mean?"

"First of all, let me assure you that your family is OK."

Jack was now fully awake and standing. "Oh, thank God. What happened?"

"Where are you located right now? Did you make it to the island?"

"No, the flight was canceled and I'm at a hotel in Hyannis. I plan to come over first thing in the morning."

"Mr. Kendrick, there's been a fire at your house, and there's pretty extensive damage. No one's been injured, and the fire is now out."

"Where's my family?"

Hines replied, "After we talked on the phone early last evening, I drove by the house a couple of times, but no one was at home. The third time I found your family in the driveway and told them about your call and that they should find somewhere else to spend the night. They said they would go to some friend's house. I came by again a while later, and even though the car was still there, they had gone."

Remembering Allison, Jack asked, "Was there another woman with my wife?"

"Yes, and I assume she went with your family."

"She's the one who sleeps in that room over the garage."

"We've checked the entire house, and there was definitely no one there."

"How did the fire start?"

"Well, they don't really know yet. It looks like it began in the garage, and there was a tremendous amount of heat generated in a short time. I was coming by on my regular half-hour swing past the house around one thirty and discovered the fire. I called the fire department, and they arrived within ten minutes. Although they got the fire out pretty quickly, there's some damage to the main part of the house, and the garage and the room overhead are pretty much destroyed. The car was still in the garage, and it's a total loss."

"Have you contacted my wife yet?"

"No, I thought I should call you first, and I really don't know where she went. I think she said she'd be with some person she works with."

"Yeah, I know who that is, and I'll call her first thing in the morning."

"I'm sorry to have to give you this news, Mr. Kendrick, but thank God your family is safe."

"Yes, and thanks for your call and for getting them out of the house." Finally remembering the reason he'd called Hines the previous evening, he said, "It sounds like this is Gimble's work. Have you had any luck finding him?"

"No. We've been tied up with the fire until now. I must have driven by the house close to ten times after you called, and I saw no evidence of anything out of the ordinary. I'll begin to check around now and see if he checked into any hotels or guesthouses. As you said when you first called, we can't be sure he's on the island, and the fire department thinks the fire might have been started from an overheated engine igniting something underneath the car. Maybe there was a leak from the gas tank."

Jack quickly replied, "Well, it's too much of a coincidence for me. I think you'll find Gimble's behind this and is somewhere on the island."

"We'll keep you informed, but in the meantime I think you and your family should take precautions. If he set the fire and is still on the island, he may find out that he didn't accomplish what he intended and try something else."

"Yeah, I agree."

"When you get on island, I'd like both you and your friend Allison to come down to the station and give us a more detailed description of this guy Gimble."

"OK, I'll call you in the morning once I get on island."

It was now close to three thirty in the morning, and Jack knew he could not get back to sleep and it was way too early to call Amy. After talking to Officer Collins, he figured she was probably at Kathy Abraham's house and Allison must be with her. But then in the next moment the fear of injury to his family returned, and he began to question whether what Officer Hines had told him was right. *Why was the car still in the garage? Did the firemen really check the house carefully to make certain no one was there? Hines said he told them to leave, so there's probably nothing to worry about, but I won't feel at ease until I hear her voice.* His mind continued to move rapidly from one thing to another. *Where is that bastard Gimble now? Could he have taken Amy and the kids somewhere and then set fire to the house? No, that doesn't make sense.*

For the next three hours, Jack alternated between pacing the room and watching CNN on the television. The minutes dragged by agonizingly slowly, more so than any waiting that Jack had done in his entire life. He made coffee in the coffeemaker; normally, the fact that the flavor was bland and not appealing would have deterred him from drinking more than a couple of sips. But tonight anything that would help pass the time was welcome.

Finally the digital clock clicked by to six o'clock, and he couldn't wait any longer to call Amy.

Kathy Abraham answered the phone, her voice clearly cautious and apprehensive about a call so early in the morning.

"Kathy, its Jack. I'm sorry to call so early, but there's been a fire at the house. Can you get Amy?"

"Of course. Give me a minute. I'm not sure she's up yet."

Less than a minute went by before Amy came on the phone. "Jack, what's wrong?"

"Hi, honey. I know it's early, but I wanted to call before you heard some other way." He continued after absorbing the relief in hearing her voice, "I got a call from the Nantucket police at about three o'clock this morning. There's been a fire at our house."

"Oh, Jack. How bad was it? Was it set?"

"I don't know the answer to either question. The police officer said the garage was badly damaged, but there was less damage to the main part of the house. We'll just have to wait and see. The police don't know whether it was set or not, but I'm sure it must be Gimble. There are too many coincidences for it to be some other reason."

"Oh my God!"

"You'll tell Allison what's happened?"

"Yes, I will. She was real upset when she listened to your voice mail about Gimble, and I know the fire will be a real shock."

"Tell her she'll have to go down to the police station with me and give a description of Gimble. He's still got to be on the island somewhere."

"OK."

"I tried to call you several times last evening. Did you get my messages?"

"Jack, my cell phone is dead. I forgot to recharge it."

"Oh! Look, Amy, I don't think it's safe for any of you to remain on the island while this guy is on the loose."

"What do you mean?"

"I think we should pack up things and go back to Quincy, and Allison should probably go back to her parents."

Amy considered everything that needed to be done before she could leave. Not only packing up the family belongings, but also probably closing up the shop. "Jack, can we talk about this more when you get here? It's too much for me to think about right now."

"OK, I understand. But look, Amy, I want you to keep the doors locked until I get there. There should be a police car somewhere near Kathy's house. Officer Hines agreed to have one outside the house after we talked a few hours ago."

Amy went to the front window and looked out to the street. "Yes, there's one right in front of the house."

"Good. Look, I'm going to try to make the six thirty flight. I'll see you in a little while. I love you."

"Me too."

54

Saturday—5:30 a.m.

Dick Gimble looked at his watch, sat up, and tried to work the many kinks out of his body from spending almost four fitful hours on the backseat of the car. Although the sun had not yet risen, he could see the brightening sky off to the east. He silently gave thanks that the rain had ended and the flight would not be delayed because of weather.

Although the car rental desk would not open until seven o'clock, he could see that the daily life of the airport was beginning to stir, and he didn't want to be found sleeping in the backseat. He went to the trunk of the car, retrieved the empty gas can, and put it back in the gym bag. He made a halfhearted attempt to straighten out his clothes and then walked the short distance over to the ACK Airlines terminal.

He went up to the check-in desk, gave the clerk the unused portion of his round-trip ticket, and was given a boarding pass. The clerk asked for his weight and took the gym bag to check it in. *I wish I didn't still have this damn gas can, but I can't take the risk of trying to get rid of it on the island.*

Gimble looked around at the other passengers and then went to take a seat against the wall. He looked at the clock, and it was now 5:40 a.m. He thought, *Twenty minutes and then I'll be off this goddamn island.*

Earlier he had thought about driving by the house to see how badly it was damaged; however, not only would it still have been dark, there was also the risk the police might still be around the area. He had convinced himself there was no way that Allison could have survived the fire.

He began to think about his plans for the day. Although he was pretty smug about what he believed he had accomplished, he was anxious for the flight to leave because there was still one more loose end he had to take care of. He had decided that Ed Fletcher presented too much of a risk after his ranting and raving the previous evening. He couldn't take the chance of Ed blowing the whole thing by shooting off his mouth.

It was a couple of minutes before six o'clock. The sun was over the horizon when the clerk called the flight, and Gimble was the first person up and at the door ready to leave the terminal. He walked the short distance to the plane with four other passengers taking this early morning flight and climbed on board.

The pilot was given the signal to start the left engine, and it coughed, sputtered, and then died. He tried again and with the same unsuccessful result. Gimble was getting a little more anxious and even began to worry about what he would do if the plane, for some reason, was not fit to fly. Finally, on the third attempt the engine caught, and then the pilot started the right-hand engine with no trouble. He then took what seemed like an inordinate amount of time revving up both engines loudly and separately. *It must be that they do this on the first flight in the morning.*

Finally, when the pilot released the brakes and the plane began to move, Gimble gave a noticeable sigh of relief. They taxied slowly out toward the runway. The pilot stopped the plane and revved up the engines one more time. He got final clearance from the tower, taxied to the end of the runway, and quickly pushed the throttles to full power. The plane accelerated down the runway and into the morning sky.

The early morning view was spectacular as they flew over the ocean along the south coast of the island for some ten miles, avoiding the shorter flight directly across the island in order to conform to the noise abatement procedures. Just as the plane passed Smith's Point, the pilot banked the plane to the north for the twenty-six-mile flight to the mainland. The sea was calm with the sun reflecting off the water, and Gimble could easily pick out some early morning fishing boats heading out toward Great Point.

In contrast to the delayed flight the previous evening, this one made the short flight to Hyannis in the scheduled time of twenty minutes. After they exited the plane, Dick waited for the luggage to be unloaded, grabbed the gym bag, and quickly moved through the terminal to the parking lot and his car. He tossed the bag in the trunk, drove to the exit, paid the overnight parking fee, and left the airport.

After he had driven over the Sagamore Bridge onto Route 3 and headed toward Boston, he opened his cell phone and called Ed Fletcher.

In a voice as casual and cheery as he could make it, he said, "Well, good morning, Ed. Hope I didn't disturb your beauty sleep."

Ed, in a muted voice and clearly distraught, said, "No, I didn't sleep at all."

"Look, Ed, I've taken care of things in Nantucket, and everything's going to be OK."

"I don't know what you're talking about, and I don't think I want to hear."

Dick hesitated only briefly and replied, "Look, I've got to go home and clean up, but I'll come by around ten o'clock and we can talk. OK?"

"Yeah, come over if you like, but I don't think there's anything to talk about, Dick. I've made up my mind, and I'm going to talk to the company Monday morning."

"Look, for Christ's sake, try and relax, will you? Everything's taken care of.

There's nothing to worry about."

Dick closed the phone and said out loud, even though there was no one to hear him, "Ed, you're the one last detail I need to take care of!"

Jack hurried to check out of the hotel and drive the short distance to the airport. This morning he took the time to park his car in the long-term parking area, but then he had to run to get to the ticket counter before the plane left. He was told the first section of the nine-passenger plane was full, but there would be a second section leaving a few minutes after six thirty.

As he sat waiting for the plane to be called, he began to think of what might have happened if he had not learned Gimble was on his way to Nantucket and he had not called the police and his family. Again his mind continued to ruminate over all the possibilities. *He must still be on the island. There wasn't enough time for him to have caught either the ferry or a plane after he set the fire. Where would he have stayed last night? His buddy Andrews is in jail, so he had to go somewhere else. Will he go by the house this morning to see what damage was done? Will he stay around to find out if he was successful in killing Allison? Will he try again? Damn it, it's too dangerous for Amy and the kids to be there. God, I hope the police are on top of this. I'm glad I told Amy that we had to get everyone off the island and back to Quincy until this whole mess is solved.*

At that moment the passengers from the six o'clock flight from Nantucket, the first ACK Airlines flight in the morning, entered the terminal and moved toward the exit. Jack casually looked up as they were passing and then briefly returned to his reading. Then, startled, he took a more careful look at the passengers. One of the men leaving the building and carrying a small satchel looked like Dick Gimble. His first thought was to go after Gimble, but he quickly realized it would be foolish to try to stop a man who had attempted murder several times in the past few months. He reached in his bag, took out his camera, and moved quickly to the exit.

He set the zoom lens on the highest reading and took several shots of Gimble as he walked toward the parking lot. When Gimble reached his car, Jack crossed the street and moved to a location behind some other cars but between Gimble and the exit. Gimble opened the trunk of the car and tossed in a carry-on bag. As he drove by, Jack felt he got a good profile shot of him, and then as the car stopped at the tollbooth, he focused on the rear number plate and took several additional shots.

He was tempted to get in his own car and follow Gimble, but he realized that the important thing for him to do was to get to his family on the island as soon as possible. He watched Gimble's car leave the parking lot and then took his cell phone and called the Nantucket police.

"Nantucket Police Department."

"Can I speak with Officer Hines?"

The clerk on the line replied, "Please give me your full name and address."

Excited and somewhat frustrated, Jack replied, "This is Jack Kendrick calling. I'm the one whose house was set on fire last evening. I'm at the airport in Hyannis, and I've just seen the man who set the fire come off a plane from Nantucket. He just left the airport parking lot, and someone there needs to arrange to have him apprehended."

"Please give me your full name and address."

"My name is Jack Kendrick. This is an emergency. Last night I talked with Officer Hines at the fire. He knows what's going on."

"Will you hold the line please while I check?" At that point his plane was called, and Jack glanced back into the waiting room and saw that passengers were exiting through a door to the tarmac.

The clerk at the police station seemed to take forever, but after a few moments she came back on the line. "Mr. Kendrick, Officer Hines is not available right now, but Detective Collins will speak with you."

Jack thought, *Oh shit. I don't need to deal with him right now. Hines has been a hell of a lot more cooperative.*

"Hello, this is Detective Collins."

"Detective, this is Jack Kendrick. Are you up to date on the fire at our house last night?"

Collins, somewhat formally, said, "Officer Hines informed me of the incident before he left; however, I just came on duty and don't have any details."

"Well, I'm at the Hyannis Airport and have just seen the man who I believe set the fire."

Collins thought for a moment before saying, "I'm not aware that it's been determined that it was arson."

"Look, Detective, you and I have talked previously about the attempts on the life of Allison Sheppard, and this was another one that almost succeeded. On top of that my house has sustained serious damage, and this guy needs to be arrested before he tries something else."

"Mr. Kendrick, I need to remind you that we can't just go off arresting people without some indication that a crime's been committed and that this person is a legitimate suspect."

Jack, now clearly showing irritation in his voice, said, "Look, Detective, my plane has just been called, and I've got to hang up. I'll call you as soon as I get to the island."

"I'll wait for your call, but there's nothing more I can do until I get more solid information."

As the announcement of the final call for his flight was made, Jack ran to the boarding area. He settled into his seat as the plane took off, trying to relax after his frustrating conversation with Detective Collins. *How does such an incompetent, arrogant bastard get to his level in the police department? I know nothing's going to happen when I call him back. Hines was a hundred percent better to deal with.*

The flight was uneventful, and he took a taxi to Kathy Abraham's house. Amy met him at the door. They embraced for several moments, and Jack looked at her and said, "Thank God you're safe!" He then went and found the children, still asleep after being up late the previous evening, and after staring at each one for moment, he bent down and gently kissed them.

Saturday—7:30 a.m.

Jack ate a couple of bagels and drank several cups of coffee while he filled Amy and Allison in on the events of the previous evening. He borrowed Kathy's car, and before he went to the police station, he drove to the house.

He sat in the driveway for a few minutes taking in the damage—the holes in the roof over the room where Allison would have been sleeping, the charred remains of the car in the garage, and the collapse of the ceiling onto the car. He looked at the main part of the house and could see some charring around the second-floor windows closest to the garage, but from the outside there seemed to be minimal damage. He thought to himself, *The garage is a total loss, but the house doesn't look bad from here. I wonder how much water and smoke damage there is. Thank God Amy and the kids weren't here. That bastard Gimble has got to be stopped.*

He drove to the police station angry, frustrated, and determined to confront Collins and convince him to call the state police on the mainland and have Gimble arrested. He was shown into an interview room, and after he'd waited almost twenty minutes, Collins walked in with a cup of coffee in his hand.

"Good morning, Mr. Kendrick. Can I get you a cup?"

"No, I've already had several. Do you have any further information on the fire last night?"

"Not really. I've read Officer Hines's notes, and I'm waiting for a report from the fire department as to what they believe is the cause."

Jack, speaking rapidly but trying to control his anger, said, "Detective, I told you over the phone I believe this guy Gimble flew down here last night with the intention of killing Allison Sheppard, and he set the fire. I believe he's also the one who arranged the accident on the bike path a couple of weeks ago and could have killed her then. It's possible he also is the one responsible for some serious injuries she received last fall. She's been investigating a case of insurance fraud at their company, and it looks to me like Gimble is behind it and is trying to get rid of her."

"Whoa, slow down a bit. Why don't you start at the beginning and tell me what you're talking about? Let me record this so I don't miss anything."

Jack spent the next ten minutes detailing Allison's bike accidents, the actuarial investigation she had initiated, his visit with Ed Fletcher the previous evening, the fact that he was quite certain he had seen Gimble get off the plane a couple of hours earlier, and his conclusion that Gimble was behind everything.

Collins spent several moments pondering what Jack had told him and finally said, "Look, you certainly put together a strong case against this guy Gimble, but I need to chase down some of this before we can arrest him."

"Even though he may be off island now, I'm really concerned about the safety of my family, as well as Allison Sheppard, until this guy is caught. I'm pretty sure the person I saw in Hyannis was him, but it's possible I was mistaken, and if so, he's probably still on the island."

"We did provide police protection for your family last night, and we'll continue to do that until we've resolved this."

"I took some photos of him leaving the Hyannis airport, and I have one of his car and the license plate." Jack pulled out his camera and enlarged the photo, but the license plate was not readable.

Collins looked at the car and said, "It looks like a Honda Civic to me, but without the plate number there's not much I can do. Do you have his address, as well as one for this guy Fletcher?"

"I was at Fletcher's last night in Natick; I have the address right here." He reached into his pocket and pulled out a piece of paper and handed it to Collins. "I don't know where Gimble lives, but I believe it's also in Natick, not far from Fletcher."

"Well, I'll check on that. You know, you should have involved the Natick or the state police rather than trying your hand at being an amateur detective. They might have prevented what happened last evening, and frankly it's damn dangerous."

Jack thought to himself, *Damn it, if I'd gotten cooperation from you earlier, I wouldn't have had to go at it myself.* Instead he simply nodded his head and asked, "Will you call the fire department while I'm here and see if they've come to any conclusions on the cause of the fire?"

Collins, at this point anxious to end the meeting, picked up the phone and called the fire chief. After a brief conversation he hung up the phone and said to Jack, "Well, they haven't reached any final conclusions yet. They think there may have been a leak in the gas tank and somehow it ignited and got the fire going. In any event, they're bringing the state fire marshal in to help in the investigation. The chief said it's going to take several days. The explosion of the gas tank doesn't help in determining the cause."

Jack stood up and said, "I'm taking my family and Allison Sheppard off the island either today or tomorrow. You have my home address in Quincy, and I'll get copies of these photos made before I leave and drop them off."

"Yeah, that may be helpful." And then, recognizing that Jack was not at all satisfied, he said, "I'm sorry we can't jump into this the way you'd like, but we have to be really careful before we make an arrest. You know nowadays we have to go really slow because of all the individual rights and privacy stuff."

Jack said, "Yeah, I suppose so."

As he left the station, he wondered why he had bothered to try to reason with Collins. He wished he had waited to talk with Officer Hines instead.

Saturday morning

Dick Gimble reached his apartment in Natick shortly after eight o'clock, shaved, showered, and had some breakfast. He felt he had a foolproof plan as to how he was going to get rid of the "Ed problem."

Several months previously Dick had been having serious difficulty sleeping. He had gone to his primary care physician, who gave him a prescription for a sedative. He had used only a couple of pills since his physical fitness obsession of not wanting to become dependent on anything took priority over the short-term benefit. After a few days, he was able to return to a more normal sleeping pattern, in spite of the growing concerns over his mounting personal problems.

He found the largely unused container of barbiturates in his medicine cabinet, took them into his kitchenette, and poured them out onto the counter. With a heavy spoon he proceeded to crush each one into a powder. He then carefully scooped the powder back into the container.

A little before nine thirty in the morning, Dick left his apartment and headed west on Route 9 toward Fletcher's apartment building, only a few miles away. He stopped at a Starbucks a short distance from his destination and ordered two grande cappuccinos, Ed Fletcher's preferred drink. Back in his car, he opened the top of one of the coffees and poured in the powder. He stirred it around to make certain it was fully dissolved and then replaced the cover. He returned to the highway and drove the final distance to Ed's apartment.

Even though he was sure Allison was no longer a problem, he knew he had to make certain Ed didn't go off the deep end and run to the police or to the company. He was plainly and simply too much of a risk. With Ed out of the way, it would be much more difficult to link Dick to the fraud scheme. The major weak link in their scheme all along had been that someone could trace back the bank account and the postal box they had used on all of the phony applications; however, both of them were in Ed's name. He was sure if he could silence Ed, then any investigation would stop there. There would be no trail to him.

When he arrived at the apartment, he found Ed still in undershorts and a T-shirt, obviously the clothes he had slept in. His hair was in disarray, and he hadn't shaved. Unwashed dishes were scattered around the kitchen area, and the entire apartment looked and smelled as if nothing had been picked up for several days. Without saying a word of greeting, Ed returned to the easy chair where he had been sitting, and Dick noticed an open bottle of vodka on the floor along with a half-full glass.

"Jesus Christ, Ed, what are you doing, drinking your breakfast?"

"Right now it's the only way I know how to deal with this god-damn nightmare."

"Look, I told you everything's going to be OK. There's not going to be any further investigation."

Ed looked at him through somewhat glazed eyes, partly from the vodka and partly from lack of sleep, and said, "I don't want to know what you've done, Dick. I'm in deep enough shit already without more of your crazy actions."

"I've brought you a cappuccino. It's a hell of a lot better for you than the booze." He handed Ed the cup with the powdered sleeping pills.

Ed said, "Thanks." He took a sip of the coffee and finally asked, "What makes you think this thing is over?"

Dick hesitated before he went further in telling him what he had done the previous night on Nantucket; however, he needed to keep him talking while he drank the coffee and the overdose of sedatives took hold. "Let's just say I saw Allison in Nantucket, and I'm certain there'll be no further investigation."

Ed, after a moment, said, "Last evening after you left I had another visitor."

"Oh yeah, who was that?"

"It was some reporter from a Boston TV station who said he was investigating claim fraud, and for Christ's sake, he knew everything about our situation."

Dick, almost spilling his own coffee, said, "What the hell are you talking about?"

"Well, he just showed up at the door, and at first he said he was doing some kind of a survey on insurance, but after he sat down, he began talking about claim fraud. He said he got to me through the mailbox number."

"What did you say to him?"

Ed, not wanting to say that he had in any way implicated Dick, took another big drink of the coffee and defensively replied, "I didn't tell him anything. I just told him I didn't know what he was talking about. After a while he left, but he certainly let me know he was going to take this further. He's going to put together some goddamn exposé on insurance fraud for his TV station."

Dick stared at Ed for several moments, thinking to himself, *Thank God my name wasn't used when we set up the postal box, and if I ever had a doubt about killing Ed, then this seals it. With him out of the way, there's no way they can trace anything back to me. They'll think he was so depressed that he committed suicide.*

Dick, noticing that the cappuccino was rapidly being consumed, knew that he needed to play along with Ed's concerns for a while longer. He said, "Thank God you didn't say anything further to him. What's his name anyway?"

Ed, slow to respond, sort of mumbled, "I don't know. I'm not even sure he told me."

Changing the subject, Dick said, "Ed, you look like hell. Maybe you ought to go back to bed." It was becoming obvious the sleeping powder was taking hold, and the combination with the vodka had accelerated the effects.

Several moments went by without anyone speaking, and finally Ed faintly mumbled, "I'm really tired." A moment later Ed's head sagged toward his chest, and then his body sort of slipped against the arm of the easy chair.

Dick sat, still drinking his own cappuccino and watching Ed carefully. He thought to himself, *I hope there's enough barbiturate in there. I really don't have any idea how much is needed to do the job. The booze ought to help. What the hell am I going to do if he's still alive?*

For the next ten minutes he simply sat there sipping his coffee and looking for any signs of life. Finally he got up, went over to Ed, and gently tried to feel his pulse in the carotid artery in the neck. After a few moments he checked the pulse rate against his watch and thought to himself, *Well, there's still a pulse, but it's pretty slow and faint.*

He walked down to the end of the room where Ed had his computer set up, took a pair of plastic gloves from his pocket, and turned the computer on. He opened up to Windows and pulled up a blank document sheet. He stood there thinking for a while, and then he went back to his chair and sat and continued to watch Ed as his breathing became more and more shallow.

After another ten minutes he went over to Ed and again felt for his pulse. He moved his fingers around the neck area on both sides trying to find a pulse beat. He then bent down to see if he could hear any breathing. *I think he's gone, but I've got to make certain.*

Again, he went back to his chair, finished his coffee, continued to look at Ed, and went over in his mind what his next steps would be. He kept checking his watch, and after another ten minutes he went over to Ed's body and went through the same steps. At this point he was convinced Ed had no signs of life, and indeed his color had begun to turn somewhat grayish.

Dick went back to the computer and began to type at the keyboard:

I simply can't go on any further. This whole fake claim scheme was my idea, and I'm the only one involved. I had some real serious money problems, but I never meant to hurt anyone. The whole thing just got out of hand. I can't face the possibility of going to prison. To my family and friends, I'm sorry.
Ed

Dick read over the statement several times and then pressed print. He left the computer on and left the paper copy on the keyboard.

One final time, he went back to assure himself that Ed was dead. By this time the corpse's color had continued to take on the appearance of death. Dick looked around the apartment, picked up his own paper cup, and left the apartment. Leaving the building by the stairwell, he walked quickly to his car and left the apartment complex.

Saturday afternoon

Later that same day Jack Kendrick called the Nantucket Police Station and again was connected to Detective Collins.

"Detective, this is Jack Kendrick, and I'm calling to let you know that my family, Allison Sheppard, and I are leaving the island on the five forty-five ferry. Have you learned anything more?"

"Well, Mr. Kendrick, I was just going to call you. First of all, I don't know anything more about the cause of your fire; however, I just got a call from the state police. After you left this morning, I called them and gave them this guy Fletcher's name and address and told them what you'd told me. They went around to his apartment this afternoon and found him dead.

Jack said incredulously, "He's dead? What happened?"

"Well, the investigation is still ongoing, but it looks like a suicide. They think he took an overdose of drugs."

"Have you found out anything about Gimble, the one I'm certain started the fire last night?"

"No, as I told you this morning, there's nothing we can do about apprehending him until we get more information. We've got to develop the facts first."

Jack asked, "Are you sure Fletcher's death was a suicide? Gimble has tried to kill before, and he almost succeeded."

"Look, Mr. Kendrick, I shouldn't be telling you this, but the state police told me they found a suicide note, and in it this guy Fletcher admits he's the one responsible for that insurance fraud scheme, and he doesn't implicate anyone else."

Jack was not to be deterred and replied, "Well, that's not what Fletcher told me. He was very clear that the fraud was Gimble's idea, and more importantly, he implicated Gimble in all of the attempts on Allison's life. You remember he's also the one who told me Gimble was going to Nantucket last night, and that's why I think he set the fire."

"Well, you know it's not unusual for a guilty person to try to shift the blame to someone else. You only have Fletcher's word that Gimble is involved. I'm certain the state police will be checking everything out. But at this point it looks like a suicide."

"Have the state police located Gimble yet?"

"Look, Mr. Kendrick, as I told you a minute ago, they have to have some more definite information before they can pick him up."

Jack, frustrated, said, "Yeah, I heard you before, but I still don't understand. There's a person out there who tried to kill my family last night, and no one's doing anything about it." After a very audible sigh he continued, "Look, on my way to the ferry I'll drop off those pictures I took of Gimble at the airport this morning. Please let me know if you learn anything else. I'm still very concerned for my family's safety, and frankly I don't understand why you're dragging your feet."

Jack hung up the phone without waiting for a reply.

59

Sunday morning

Dick Gimble spent the rest of Saturday trying to keep occupied and periodically listened to the news to learn if there was a report of the fire or if anyone had found Ed Fletcher's body. By late evening there was still no report of either, and he was especially concerned and confused there was no information at all about the Nantucket fire. *It's been almost twenty-four hours, and any fire with a death ought to make the Boston news, even if it was on Nantucket. Is it possible that she got out alive, and therefore it's not so much of a story? As far as Fletcher is concerned, probably no one's found his body yet.*

He slept fitfully all night and went to the corner convenience store as soon as it opened at seven o'clock and bought copies of the *Boston Globe* and the *Middlesex News.* He sat in his car and quickly found articles in both papers about Fletcher's death. Both reports were quite vague, saying that he had been found dead in his apartment and that "the cause of death is unknown, but an autopsy will be performed."

He went through both papers carefully but could find no reports of a house fire on Nantucket. He drove home and decided to go on the Internet to find any further information. He found the Web sites for both of the Nantucket papers, the *Inquirer and Mirror* and the *Independent*, but both papers were published only weekly and their next issues would not be out until the middle of the following week. He finally located a Web site for the *Cape Cod Times*, and in it he found a section for "Island News" in their Sunday edition. He found a short article on the house fire with the headline, "House Fire Damages Summer Home."

> The Nantucket Fire Department responded to a fire at the summer residence of Jack and Amy Kendrick located off of Madaket Road shortly after 1:30 a.m. Saturday. There was extensive damage to the garage and a bedroom over the garage, and smoke and water damage to the rest of the house. There was no one in the house at the time. It appears the fire started in the garage, where an automobile was destroyed. The fire marshal will be investigating the cause of the fire.

Dick sat staring at the screen, dumfounded over the report of no one found in the house. He thought to himself, *Goddamn it, there were lights on it the house earlier. I'm sure they were there. The car was in the garage. I can't believe this. Three times I've tried to get rid of her. She's like a damn cat with nine lives. Jesus Christ, what do I do now?*

As he calmed down somewhat, he began to rationalize that perhaps Ed Fletcher's death and the suicide note may truly be the end of Allison's actuarial investigation into the fraud scheme. The police and the company should conclude that Fletcher had acted alone, and as long as the phony claims stopped, then they'd believe that was the end of it. Fletcher could be traced to both the bank account and the post office box, but he didn't think there was any way to directly link to him. The only thing he feared was that there had been transfers of money out of the account to his bank account regularly over the past several years, but hopefully, with Fletcher's death the investigation wouldn't go that far.

As the day went on, he felt more and more confident that he had escaped by the skin of his teeth. He'd go to work next week and keep his eyes and ears open for any comments about Fletcher's death. That was surely to be the topic of conversation for some time, and since people knew Ed was a friend of his, they would be curious as to what he knew. *I'll have to be very careful about what I say. I've got to wait for the police or the news reports about the details before I say anything about either his suicide or his suicide note. I don't know how much the police will release, but eventually the word will get around. Up until that point I've got to play dumb.*

He had heard early the previous week that Allison Sheppard might be returning to work after Labor Day. He'd have to check on that and casually find out exactly what happened with the fire. *Goddamn it, I can't believe she's still around. She may be one of the first ones to learn about Fletcher admitting to the fraud scheme in the suicide note. I'll have to stay close to her to find out if she's stopped her work on the actuarial study.*

Eighteen days later

Jack Kendrick was sitting in his home in Quincy on this Thursday evening having a serious discussion with Amy and Allison, who had stayed with them since returning from the island. It was Labor Day weekend, and Allison had just announced she was going back to her own apartment the next day and returning to work on Tuesday.

Jack said, "Allison, I'd really like to see you wait another couple of weeks until we clear up some of the questions we still have about Gimble. If he's involved in this whole thing, and I think he is, then it's dangerous for you to be going back to work where he is so close by, not to mention the risk of living alone in that apartment."

"Jack, I appreciate your concern and everything you and Amy have done for me over the past several weeks, but I've got to try to get my life back to normal. I know how strongly you feel about Dick Gimble, but we can't really be sure he has been involved in any way. The police haven't come up with anything that ties him into either the fraud scheme or the accidents."

"I know it's got to be very frustrating for you, but I still believe someone tried to kill you three times, and the likely one responsible is Gimble."

"I really have considered everything you say, but I've got to get on with my life. I can't let some unknown fear rule my every day. I've been on hold for almost a whole year now, and I've got to take charge of my own destiny."

Early the next morning, Allison packed her few belongings in her car and returned to her apartment in Upton.

Jack went off to work at the store that morning in Quincy Market but couldn't concentrate. He kept thinking back over the whole problem. He had called the Nantucket police twice since his return to his home on the mainland, but they said nothing further had developed. Each time he had talked with Al Collins, and he finally was convinced he was being given the brush-off.

He decided to call one more time and was relieved to find Officer Hines was on duty, and the call was quickly transferred to him.

"Hello, Mr. Kendrick, this is Dick Hines. How can I help you?"

"Hello, Officer. I'm calling to find out if you've learned anything more about the cause of my fire and also if you've heard anything further from the state police about Ed Fletcher's suicide. I've called Al Collins a couple of times, but he didn't have any ad-
-ditional information."

Jack then said, "Allison Sheppard plans to go back to work next week, and she'll be in close contact with this guy Gimble, and I'm frankly worried."

Jack could hear Hines shuffling some papers, and then Hines replied, "We just received the final report from the fire marshal's office about the cause of your fire, and they still think it was probably accidental. They didn't rule out some other reason, but they said the combination of a probable fuel leak from the gas tank and an overheated engine was the likely cause. Their report states, 'We did not find any conclusive evidence to cause us to suspect any other cause, including arson, as the reason for the fire.' I'm afraid at this point we can't go any further with our investigation."

"What do they mean by 'any conclusive evidence'? Sounds like they're saying there might be another reason."

"Well, that's sort of common language when they can't find definitive evidence as to the cause. Even though they feel that it was accidental, they're leaving the door open to some other possibility."

Jack then asked, "How about Fletcher's suicide?"

"I was going to get to that. I actually called the state police in Framingham yesterday and talked to an officer I know pretty well. Normally they're hesitant to give out any details, but he read me the investigating officer's report, and it had some interesting things in it."

"What do you mean?"

"Well, first of all, they're still claiming it was suicide. Everything points to that—the sleeping pills and, of course, the suicide note. But what was interesting to me was some of the detail in the report. For example, they mention that they found the Starbucks coffee cup, and the lab report says it had traces of the sleeping pills and cappuccino coffee. Then they go on to mention that this was consistent with what the autopsy found in Fletcher's system, but then, sort of in passing, the report mentioned a couple of other things. First, they said there was a container of sleeping pills found in Fletcher's medicine cabinet that was almost full. And second, they said they could not find an empty container for the pills that he must have put in his cappuccino. Finally the report questions why there was evidence of the barbiturate in the coffee cup. Wouldn't he have swallowed the pills and then washed them down with the cappuccino?"

Jack was alert to what Hines was implying and said, "So you're wondering why Fletcher didn't use the pills in his medicine cabinet, and also where was the container for the ones he used?"

"Yeah, right."

"Well, what does the report conclude?"

"It doesn't say anything further. I asked my friend about it, and even though they may have those questions, they're still saying it was suicide."

"Christ, what do they need to consider the fact that it may have been murder?"

"Well, that's a big leap for them at this point. The suicide note sort of overrides any of the other questions, especially since it's clear Fletcher was definitely involved in the insurance fraud, and they've traced both the bank account and the postal box that was used in the fraud to him."

"Yeah, I'm aware of that. But Fletcher told me the evening before he died that Gimble was the mastermind behind the fraud scheme."

"I know what you told us he said, and we did pass that on to the state police, but apparently they think he was trying to shift the blame."

Hines then said, "There is one thing more."

"What's that?"

"Well, the report says that Fletcher was wearing only shorts and a T-shirt, and they concluded that those were probably the clothes he slept in."

Waiting for Hines to continue, Jack asked, "Yeah, what else?"

"The report doesn't say anything more, but I've been thinking about this further, and it doesn't make sense that Fletcher was still in his sleeping clothes if he had gone out and gotten a cappuccino from Starbucks."

"You mean, someone brought it to him, like Gimble?"

"Right."

"And that means someone could have put the drugs in the coffee with the intent to kill him?"

"That's what I'm thinking, but I must caution you that there may be some other logical explanation we're not considering."

Ignoring Hines's last comment, Jack's mind was racing even further. "And that same person could have sat down at Fletcher's computer and typed the suicide note."

"Well, that's one scenario."

"Shouldn't there be some fingerprints on the note or on the computer?"

"You'd think so—unless the killer was wearing gloves."

"Have you asked the state police about this?"

"No, not yet. I only thought about this last night. I plan to call the state trooper I talked to and see what he says."

"I think you've really come up with enough questions for them to reopen the investigation."

"Well, we'll see. They really don't particularly care for anyone interfering with their investigations. There may be another explanation for the coffee cup and the sleeping pills that we haven't thought of. I'll let you know if I learn anything more. In the meantime, I think your friend should be really careful."

"Yeah, I agree, and thanks for the information and for sharing your thoughts with me. Please tell the state police I'm available anytime if they want to talk with me."

As Jack hung up the phone, he thought to himself, *Now, that's what I call a real thinking investigator. He's not just taking things as fact, but he's using his own head to consider other possibilities. Why isn't he heading up this investigation rather than Collins?*

61

Later that same day

Jack spent the rest of the day thinking about his conversation with Officer Hines. He was more certain than ever that Gimble was behind the insurance fraud and also had tried to kill Allison on those three separate occasions, and after talking with Hines, he was increasingly sure that Gimble had something to do with Fletcher's death. He tried to call Allison at her apartment several times but without any luck.

He was afraid when Officer Hines went to the state police they'd either discount what he'd concluded, or they would drag their feet for weeks before anything further was done. It seemed as though once the state police had made up their mind on something, it took an act of Congress to get them to consider something else. He thought Al Collins probably wouldn't give much weight to what Hines had concluded, and even if he did, it wasn't likely he'd have any more clout with the state police.

Something had to be done to bring this whole crazy mess to a conclusion, and by the end of the day he had decided he would put a little pressure on Dick Gimble that evening. After work he drove out to Natick to Gimble's apartment building, found his car in the parking lot, and parked in a spot where he had good visibility. He then took his cell phone, dialed information, got Gimble's number, and placed the call.

After a couple of rings, Gimble answered the phone. "Hello."

"Is this Richard Gimble?"

"Yes, who's calling?"

"I'm an investigative reporter with WBOS-TV, and I'm calling to get your reaction to a special investigative report that will be aired on our station tomorrow evening. It has to do with insurance fraud and is based upon information we've uncovered during the past several weeks."

As Jack paused, Gimble said, "Yeah, what does that have to do with me?"

"Well, the report will implicate you, Mr. Gimble, as the mastermind of a claim fraud scheme at the John Adams Insurance Company."

"You're crazy!"

"A friend of yours, Ed Fletcher, implicated you before he died a couple of weeks ago."

Almost too quickly, Gimble replied, "Fletcher must have been trying to shift the blame to someone else. I had nothing to do with it. I heard he even left a suicide note saying he was responsible."

"Well, notes can be forged. I met personally with Mr. Fletcher the evening before he died, and he clearly implicated you. Also, the report will suggest you may be responsible for several attempts on the life of a person by the name of Allison Sheppard, an employee of the company. Do you have anything to say about that?"

"Look Mr. Whatever-your-name-is, this is bullshit. I have nothing to do with any claim fraud, and Allison Sheppard is a friend of mine. I would never try to harm her." As his anxiety rose, he said, "If those charges are made in the press or on TV, then you and your station are going to be sued."

"We don't proceed with a report like this unless we're absolutely sure of our information." Jack then took a risk with the facts and said, "Also, you were captured on a security camera at both the Nantucket and Hyannis airports the morning after a fire was set in the latest attempt to murder Ms. Sheppard."

Gimble was physically shaking as he said, "This is some kind of a goddamn frame-up, and I'm not going to listen to this shit any longer."

Jack asked, "Mr. Gimble, I take it you deny all of my allegations?"

"You bet your ass I do, and I'll have your ass if you go ahead with this report."

Jack said, "Good-bye, Mr. Gimble," and he hung up.

After Dick Gimble hung up the phone, he continued to stare at it and tried to control his physical shaking. He went to a cupboard in the kitchen, pulled down a bottle of whiskey, and poured himself a large tumbler full of the amber liquid. He didn't even bother to add ice. He paced back and forth, trying to calm down and make some sense out of the call. *That weak son of a bitch Fletcher didn't say anything about having given my name to the reporter who came to his apartment. I wonder if this guy was just fishing and if they're really going ahead with this story.*

He took several large gulps of the alcohol and felt its warmth as it settled into his system. He continued to pace back and forth. *They're only going on Fletcher's say-so, and the suicide note said that he alone* was behind the phony claims. *The more I think about it, the more I wonder if he was trying to get me to admit something and that they really don't have enough to publish the story.*

He poured some more whiskey into the tumbler, took a couple of more large swallows, and continued to anguish over the call. *Jesus Christ, the thing that really scares me is his asking me about Allison's accidents. Did that fool Fletcher mention Allison? And then, he mentioned the surveillance photos at the airport. I wonder if they've contacted Allison about the accidents. I wonder what she thinks.*

As he continued to try to think through the implications of the reporter's comments, the alcohol had the effect of somewhat calming his anxiety, even though his thoughts were becoming scattered. *I still think he was fishing and trying to trap me. The key to this whole goddamn mess right now is Allison. In the note I wrote, Fletcher said that he alone was behind the claim fraud, so I don't think anyone has a leg to stand on there. But I've got to get to Allison before anyone suggests to her that I was behind the accidents.*

He took one last long swig and finished the glass, grabbed his car keys, and left the apartment. He spun his wheels as he left the parking lot and headed west on Route 9.

After a few miles he turned south on Route 135 and headed toward the town of Upton and Allison's apartment. He had decided it would be better to arrive unannounced than call her in advance.

With each passing mile his thinking became more muddled and his physical reactions became more sluggish. As he left Framingham and the highway took him through Ashland and Hopkinton, the road became less populated and more wooded. He had picked up his speed well beyond the posted speed limit as his anxiety continued to escalate. *I've got to convince Allison I had nothing to do with either the claim fraud or the accidents. Jesus, I've got to be real careful.*

At a sharp bend in the road he overcorrected for the turn and sharply pulled the steering wheel to get the car back on the right side of the road, and as he came through the curve, two bikers were

62

After Dick Gimble hung up the phone, he continued to stare at it and tried to control his physical shaking. He went to a cupboard in the kitchen, pulled down a bottle of whiskey, and poured himself a large tumbler full of the amber liquid. He didn't even bother to add ice. He paced back and forth, trying to calm down and make some sense out of the call. *That weak son of a bitch Fletcher didn't say anything about having given my name to the reporter who came to his apartment. I wonder if this guy was just fishing and if they're really going ahead with this story.*

He took several large gulps of the alcohol and felt its warmth as it settled into his system. He continued to pace back and forth. *They're only going on Fletcher's say-so, and the suicide note said that he alone* was behind the phony claims. *The more I think about it, the more I wonder if he was trying to get me to admit something and that they really don't have enough to publish the story.*

He poured some more whiskey into the tumbler, took a couple of more large swallows, and continued to anguish over the call. *Jesus Christ, the thing that really scares me is his asking me about Allison's accidents. Did that fool Fletcher mention Allison? And then, he mentioned the surveillance photos at the airport. I wonder if they've contacted Allison about the accidents. I wonder what she thinks.*

As he continued to try to think through the implications of the reporter's comments, the alcohol had the effect of somewhat calming his anxiety, even though his thoughts were becoming scattered. *I still think he was fishing and trying to trap me. The key to this whole goddamn mess right now is Allison. In the note I wrote, Fletcher said that he alone was behind the claim fraud, so I don't think anyone has a leg to stand on there. But I've got to get to Allison before anyone suggests to her that I was behind the accidents.*

He took one last long swig and finished the glass, grabbed his car keys, and left the apartment. He spun his wheels as he left the parking lot and headed west on Route 9.

After a few miles he turned south on Route 135 and headed toward the town of Upton and Allison's apartment. He had decided it would be better to arrive unannounced than call her in advance.

With each passing mile his thinking became more muddled and his physical reactions became more sluggish. As he left Framingham and the highway took him through Ashland and Hopkinton, the road became less populated and more wooded. He had picked up his speed well beyond the posted speed limit as his anxiety continued to escalate. *I've got to convince Allison I had nothing to do with either the claim fraud or the accidents. Jesus, I've got to be real careful.*

At a sharp bend in the road he overcorrected for the turn and sharply pulled the steering wheel to get the car back on the right side of the road, and as he came through the curve, two bikers were coming toward him at a fast pace. Gimble's automatic but impaired reactions caused him to quickly jerk the wheel again to avoid the bikers, but his overreaction and his speed resulted in the car going out of control and flipping over three times before it came to rest against a tree.

Gimble, either because of his inebriated state or his macho personality, had failed to fasten his seat belt and was thrown from the car and pinned under it. The trunk of the car sprang open, and a canvas gym bag was thrown onto the highway.

Another auto following Gimble observed the entire event, and the driver took out his cell phone and immediately called 911. The bikers had quickly stopped and tried to aid Gimble, but they realized there was clearly nothing they could do for him. One of the bikers then went to retrieve the gym bag in the road and noticed the baggage tag that read "ACK Airlines."

POSTSCRIPT

Dick Gimble was declared dead at the scene of the accident. Over the next several days the Upton police, after discussions with the state police and eventually the Nantucket police, learned more about the suspicions surrounding Gimble. The gym bag and the empty gas can inside were turned over to Al Collins in Nantucket. The ACK Airlines tag number was traced back to the flight from Nantucket to Hyannis the morning after the house fire, and consequently the official cause of the fire was changed to arson.

Ed Fletcher was buried at a private memorial service attended by his family alone. Although there was no further evidence to suggest his death was anything but suicide, the final police report left open the strong possibility that Gimble was somehow involved.

Tony Andrews was tried for multiple charges of drug trafficking, receiving stolen property, and being an accessory to attempted murder. He was sentenced to thirty years in prison at Walpole. His business was seized by the state, and the property, along with all of the secondhand merchandise, was sold and the proceeds used to reimburse those whose property had been stolen.

Phil Costa, the drug addict who had tried to injure Allison on the bike path, turned state's evidence and was sentenced to fifteen years for attempted murder. He also implicated more than a dozen other island residents and drug addicts who took part in the ring that stole the electronics merchandise and traded it to Tony Andrews for drugs. The state sought and got convictions on all but two of those Costa had identified.

The town of Nantucket experienced a sharp drop in drug-related problems and crimes following the conviction of Tony Andrews; however, within a year the drug trafficking had once again returned to its previous level.

Detective Al Collins received a commendation from the state police for breaking up the drug ring on the island. The local newspapers carried pictures of him on the front page and credited him with not only breaking up the drug ring, but also solving the multiple house break-ins and even the claim fraud scheme at John Adams Insurance Company. In the numerous interviews that Collins had, including one with WBOS-TV, he consistently embellished his own role in the investigations and never mentioned the significant part that Officer Dick Hines and Jack Kendrick played in breaking the cases wide open.

Allison Sheppard returned to work at the John Adams Insurance Company to her position in the actuarial department. Her first assignment from her boss was to complete the claim fraud study. During her investigation, she also uncovered the second fraud scheme of Gimble's where he had reinstated dozens of lapsed policies and then submitted more phony claims. She estimated that the total loss to the company from both schemes was in excess of six hundred thousand dollars. It took several months before her anger began to abate over having been hoodwinked by Dick Gimble. She enmeshed herself in studying for her final actuarial exams and two years later became a Fellow of the Society of Actuaries.

The John Adams Insurance Company made substantial changes in both its underwriting rules and its claim examination practices to hopefully prevent a recurrence of similar fraud schemes. It hired a few more claim examiners to focus more attention on new claims on recently approved policies; however, at the same time, its management was well aware that the potential for someone to pocket tens of thousands of dollars would always be an incentive for fraud.

Amy Kendrick closed her photography store on Nantucket after Labor Day. The season had been successful, and she was making plans with Kathy Abraham to expand their operation during the next year. She was very busy during the following several months, however, overseeing the repairs to the Nantucket home. The garage and room overhead had to be entirely rebuilt, and even though the damage to the main house had been minimal, she took the opportunity to make some renovations. The insurance proceeds paid most of the cost of the repairs, and the income from the Nantucket store made up the difference.

Jack Kendrick continued to manage the Faneuil Hall photography store. If you visited the store periodically, you'd find that the pictures and displays changed regularly. He continued to look for new subjects and new scenes, and he enjoyed and took great pride in always finding ways to improve the merchandise he offered to the public. For relaxation he continued to read mysteries, but he had to admit to friends that his own experiences during the past couple of years were more exciting and in many ways more unbelievable than most of the novels he read.

5235434R0

Made in the USA
Charleston, SC
18 May 2010